P9-BXW-700

Waiting to Score

For Larry and Max Gurtler
who made writing this story possible.

Waiting to Score

J.E. MacLeod

WestSide Books

Published by WestSide Books
60 Industrial Road
Lodi, NJ 07644
973-458-0485
Fax: 973-458-5289

Library of Congress Control Number: 2008911810

International Standard Book Number: 978-1-934813-01-0
Cover illustration Copyright © by Rick Lieder
Cover design by David Lemanowicz
Interior design by Chinedum Chukwu

Printed in the United States of America
10 9 8 7 6 5 4 3 2 1

First Edition

Waiting to Score

CHAPTER 1

I didn't want to look up. Didn't want to care. But I did. I shifted my gaze over as I untied my skates. This guy kept staring at me from across the locker room, his navy boxers blending in with the chipped blue paint on the bench. He pulled off his shoulder pads and continued to stare. I shook my head and returned to my skate laces.

He tossed his pads on the cement floor and stood. I braced myself, but then he grinned. "So. You throw a pretty good body check, Zack Attack."

A new nickname. Not a bad thing, but I didn't drop my guard as I tugged off my skates. I delivered the tough guy look I'd perfected in front of my bathroom mirror. I practice some weird-ass things in the privacy of my own home. Wherever home happens to be—this year.

"Hey, man, lighten up. You were awesome out there. I got tired trying to keep up." He stretched and grabbed a wrinkly Nike T-shirt from his bag.

I watched him smile. He didn't look vindictive. Just nosy. He sat again, and started to pull on his blue jeans.

I glanced around the locker room while I pulled my own clothes from my hockey bag. Yellowish paint flaked off the walls. The benches were old and carved up with graffiti. It smelled like crap. This was the locker room I'd spend many hours over the coming hockey season. Call me picky, but I didn't care for it much.

"How come this arena doesn't even have showers?" I asked.

"I don't know. I guess we like our boys rancid in Haletown. Don't worry, I'm sure you'll have all the showers you want in your future." He studied me, as if I were a curious science experiment that may or may not have gone wrong.

I stared back, careful not to reveal anything.

Then he grinned. Winked. "Hey. Come on. You? NHL. Name in glaring lights and all that."

"Don't hold your breath."

He rolled his eyes and turned away, probably writing me off as arrogant. I studied him for a second.

"My mom's the one who wants it so badly," I told him, surprising myself. Usually I don't tell people about that.

"Your mom's hot. She a lesbian? We have another lesbian in town." He sounded hopeful. "That other lady her girlfriend?"

"My mom is not hot. Or a lesbian. The other lady is my aunt—her sister."

Aunt Diane would laugh if she heard. A lesbian. She'd crack up. Mom would love being called hot. Gross.

"Your dad died a long time ago," he said.

I didn't answer, since he didn't sound like he wanted a response. People knew about my dad. How he died.

"You're going to make the team, you know. Don't worry about the extra drills. Coach Cal likes a little attitude." He started stuffing equipment into his hockey bag.

I nodded, pretty sure I would make the team too, no matter who made the real decisions in this particular hockey league, or what the parents wanted. I'd broken a sweat to prove myself in the tryouts, poured it on to wow the guys a little. And the coach. At one point during a quick shift change, I'd flown off the bench, caught the center, stole the puck, and poked it in the net before the goalie even blinked.

They knew they were dealing with the son of a legend now. Hockey flowed in my veins. I tried to deny it sometimes, but the call lingered in my gut, even when I wasn't on the ice. I didn't see the point in talking about it, though.

"I don't see *your* parents anywhere. Why you so interested in mine?" I asked.

He laughed. "My parents don't actually watch any of my practices. Or even my games. They work. A lot." He grinned. "My name's David."

"Lucky you."

David laughed out loud, walked over and held out his hand. We clunked knuckles. "Yeah. Lucky me. Listen, man. Sorry about the high-stick thing. Have to test the new talent out sometimes. Captain's orders. We cool?"

I lifted a shoulder. I didn't know his agenda yet. Or Mac's—the team captain.

David picked up his hockey bag and slung it over his shoulder. "Must suck being the new kid."

"Could be worse." Like I could be five two and skinny, instead of over six feet, with good hair and smoking hockey skills. I don't generally brag, but I know. It gives me built-in acceptability, at least on the fringes.

David shifted his feet to balance the weight of the hockey bag. He tilted his head and nodded. "Cool." He turned to go. "See ya 'round, Zack Attack."

I sat in the quiet room, breathing. The other guys cleared out twenty minutes earlier, while David and I did extra drills— punishment for our on-ice scrap. I concentrated, replaying in my mind the final on-ice scrimmage with my new teammates. I'd picked off the puck from a bad pass and carried it down the ice, two guys on me. After faking out one defenseman, I used the other to screen the goalie, and then I flicked the puck, placing it right in the top shelf of the net.

My stick smoked. Mac's knack for hitting my sweet spot was almost poetic. Too bad he hated passing—and me. I knew his type. Threatened by real talent. If he'd work with me instead of against me, it would make for an interesting year for both of us. But I had my doubts. Too bad. On-ice chemistry is kind of like finding the perfect girl to hook up with. You can make do with others, but when you connect with the right one, there's nothing like it.

Coach Cal popped his balding head in the locker room just then, interrupting my thoughts. He clutched a clipboard close to his Haletown Husky jacket, as if lurkers might read the notes he'd jotted down about the practice. "What are you doing? They want to close up."

"Two minutes."

He nodded. "You looked good out there, kid. Try and stay out of trouble in the future." He ducked back out the door.

Reluctantly, I got up and left the solitude. Mom and Aunt Diane hovered near the locker room door. The arena smelled like they all do. Of popcorn and sweat.

"So. Did the coach say anything?" Mom rushed forward, grabbing at my equipment bag as if to take it from me.

I glared down at her. I tower over her by a foot, and outweigh her by at least forty pounds. Yet she still wanted to carry my equipment for me.

"Mom. I got it."

"So, you going to make the team, Zachary?" Aunt Diane punched me on the arm, bouncing with excitement about me playing on her home team, smack in the middle of small-town Montana.

I rolled the hockey bag off my shoulder and threw it on the ground. "I'm going to get a Coke, okay?"

Aunt Diane started to follow me towards the concession, but Mom grabbed her by the arm and held her back.

"Of course he'll make the team, Diane. He just needs some space. He's the new kid again. He's probably nervous about fitting in," I heard her say.

I didn't bother looking back or trying to contradict them. I wasn't nervous. What was the point? I'd worked it. Besides, moving was old. Hockey players were pretty much the same everywhere. Pretty much. Mac, the captain, already hated me and I hadn't met anyone I could relate to yet, except maybe David, and he'd high-sticked me.

I headed to the concession stand in search of something to quench my thirst, my head down. My thoughts drifted to what I'd left behind. Claire. I missed her, despite everything. But I would never call her. We were over. Very over.

"Ouch! Hey, watch it," a female voice yelped.

It caught me off guard for a second, until I looked up. I'd crashed straight into a girl. She held a book open and obviously hadn't been paying attention either. She almost pierced my skin with the expression in her eyes.

I couldn't help smiling. She looked scrappy. She wasn't tiny, maybe five six, but in spite of her height, she appeared small. Thin. Maybe 110 pounds on a bloated day. Her clothes hung on her, like she'd raided her big sister's closet. Her much bigger sister. She wore a long black skirt, black Doc Martens, and a black sweater that hung on her thin shoulders, where her black hair, obviously straight from a bottle, rested.

Everything about her reeked rebel. I looked at her eyes. They glared, flashing with distaste, but they were a crazy pale blue color, kind of shiny, almost gentle, even with all the thick black eyeliner around each eye. Not a pothead, I guessed; just making a fashion statement, maybe? Even her harsh clothes, hair, and makeup couldn't disguise the good looks this girl had been born with.

She clutched a thick novel, the fold about half way through it. I tried to see the title but I couldn't make it out. "What are you reading?"

"A book," she snapped, moving it out of my sight.

"Which one? I read too, you know." I tried to see her book again, but she tucked it under her arm.

What she didn't know was that I love to read. Always have. It's my escape from the world when I'm bored. Some kids do video games; I prefer a more intellectual pastime.

She stared at me like I was a big self-absorbed jock tormenting a mere mortal. For a moment I wanted to reach up and make sure my bangs covered the scar on my forehead. A train accident—Thomas the Tank Engine, actually. He was in my hand when I tripped down the stairs when I was four. Lots of blood and screaming. Five stitches and a permanent scar.

"Nothing that would interest you," she snapped. "My IQ is bigger than my shoe size, you know. Excuse me, I need to get by."

I couldn't help it—I laughed and peeked at her feet. "I hope so."

She scrunched her eyes at me. Then she pulled her book from under her arm and shoved it towards me, showing me the title. *The Fountainhead.*

I laughed again as she tucked it back under her arm. She was funny, in a refreshing sort of way. Even I get a little sick of the kind of girls who usually hang around hockey rinks. We called them Pucks in Kirkdale. Blondes and brunettes with tight clothes and made-up eyes. Pucks, hockey groupies, whatever. I kind of thought girls should have better things to do with their time. Giggling and hanging around boys who weren't very nice to them didn't strike me as overly ambitious.

I guess snagging a hockey player for a boyfriend can heighten the social status for some girls. Most of those girls don't get boyfriends though. They just get used. Maybe they even get a disease. Gross. I couldn't imagine falling for a girl like that.

"I've read that book," I told her.

She stared at me with black-rimmed eyes. I didn't have to ask to know that she thought I was lying.

"How come you think I'm dumb?" I asked, grinning because I know for a fact that the opposite is true.

Her eyes went from the tip of my head to the Converse high-top runners I left unlaced on my overgrown feet. I reached up and adjusted my bangs.

"Good one." She stormed off.

I watched her go, and then a voice behind me spoke.

"Sorry about my sister," David said. "She hates hockey players."

"No kidding." I watched her stomp away. I could kind of relate sometimes. "How come?" I turned to look at him.

He shrugged, as if the reason was not only unimportant but also uninteresting.

"What's she doing at a hockey rink then, if she hates hockey so much?"

"My parents make her come. She has to drive me." He smiled down at his feet for a moment. "I lost my license. You know. Drinking." He grinned again. "She's the family presence, I guess. Since they're always so busy. She's been hanging out in hockey rinks since we were little kids." He peered after her. "I'd say she's pissed off."

I nodded and continued to the concession stand. I ordered a Coke from the girl behind the counter. David followed me.

"She's my twin."

I looked at him. Blond hair. Blue eyes. He was a couple inches shorter than me, but broader. Wholesome jock, through and through. I glanced to where his sister had disappeared.

"I think they switched her with another baby at birth," he said.

I nodded in agreement.

"What's her name?" I kept my voice flat, uninterested.

"Jane."

I hid my smile. She didn't look like a Jane. "She go to Jefferson High?"

"Yup. Hangs out with a freak though. She's 'literary.' It's kind of embarrassing. But, she's my sister, so what can you do?"

I had no idea. Being an only child has advantages and disadvantages. Sibling rivalry, or even sibling tolerance, was not something I understood from experience. A lot of things I had to learn on my own.

The redhead at the concession stand handed me a Coke, batted her eyelashes, and gave me a bright, big-toothed smile. "On the house," she said.

Behind me, David groaned. "Cut the crap, Sheila. He's not going out with you just because you gave him a free drink."

The girl's face fell and she turned a color close to her hair shade.

"Shut up, David." She turned and hurried away from the counter, her auburn curls swinging back and forth down her back.

"Hey, I need a drink, too!" he shouted.

She raised her middle finger up behind her round backside. She wore a pair of low-rise jeans and her hips flowed over the top of the pants.

He shrugged at me. "Serves me right for sleeping with the help."

I raised my eyebrows and glanced behind the counter at Sheila as she frantically wiped at the drink machine. She didn't seem like his type. A little plump, with wild red curls, definitely cute but she wasn't the Barbie doll type I imagined David taking out. Sheila ignored us, moving to shuffle around some chocolate bars as far away from us as she could be. She glanced up and I smiled at her, raising my Coke cup in a toast. She blushed again and kept busy. I felt a little sorry for her. Probably a nice enough girl, just trying to fit in.

David's attention moved to a group of girls standing by the arena entrance. Three of them. Skinny. Tall. Not dressed warmly enough for a freezing hockey rink. They all sported tiny T-shirts and jeans with oversized belts. Long hair. Two brunettes, one stunning blonde.

"There's my sweet Candy." He made a weird slurping noise. "Duty calls, Zack. See ya." He swaggered towards the girls.

The blonde played with her hair and preened even more as he approached.

"That's Candy Clark," said Sheila from behind me. "David has the hots for her."

I turned to look at her. She'd moved back to the counter. I took a sip of my drink and glanced back, watching David plant a kiss on Candy's cheek while she fidgeted. The other girls attempted to look uninterested, despite being completely aware of the attention they were getting from most of the adults and kids in the area.

"Mona's the resident slut at Jefferson High, and Carly is the queen," Sheila told me.

"And you're the town gossip?" I turned back to her, grinning. She leaned against the counter watching David and the girls, totally ignoring my dig.

"I'm Zack."

"I know." She didn't look at me.

One thing about being the new guy, everyone seems to know who I am.

"You're the best hockey player on the team," she told me, still watching David and Candy.

I grinned, but didn't disagree. "You know already?"

She finally looked me in the eyes and smiled back. "I've been working here since I was thirteen. You're the best hockey player I've ever seen."

"Thanks. I've been playing since I was a kid. My dad played, too. I guess it's in my blood."

She smiled again. Her grin was crooked, her mouth turned up more on the right, but she was pretty in an offbeat way.

"I know that, too. Jeremy Chase."

I nodded. My dad. Jeremy Chase. NHL star in the early '90s. All-around hero, except he'd screwed my mom.

"Anything else you know about me?"

"You play guitar. Oh, and you got your heart broken by some girl in some other small-town U.S.A."

I laughed out loud. "And where did you hear all that?"

She shrugged. "Word gets around. My sister shops at your aunt's store, where your mom works." She glanced over to my mom and aunt, deep in conversation close to David and the girls.

I raised my brows and followed her glance. "Well, don't believe everything you hear," I told her, though to be honest, so far everything she'd heard had been right. I looked to the right of my mom, where David nuzzled Candy's neck.

Jane approached David from behind, scowling at the three girls who were watching her advance. I didn't notice I was smiling her way, not until Sheila not so subtly pointed it out.

"You got a thing for bad girls, Zack? You look like you're going to leave a puddle of drool on the floor."

"Hardly." I paused. "Is Jane a bad girl?"

"Well, look at her." She gestured her head towards Jane.

"Looks are deceiving…that's what my mom always tells me."

"Your mom?"

I didn't answer, but I wasn't embarrassed by my relationship with my mom. She's one of my favorite people in the world. Didn't matter to me that I was supposed to hate her at my age. Sometimes she pissed me off, the way she talked about hockey as if it were the most important thing in life. And then there was her refusal to see the truth sometimes. But mostly she's my rock.

"Jane is totally dark. She hasn't worn anything besides black since eighth grade. And, all she ever does is read at the rink." Sheila shook her head.

"I don't think that makes her bad."

"Morose then." Sheila's eyes squinted suspiciously.

"Nothing wrong with angst. We're teenagers, right?"

She blinked at me. "You for real, Zack?"

"That's what they tell me. You for real, Sheila?"

She stuck her tongue out at me. I laughed.

I liked her. She was blunt and got points for not being afraid to use big words. Vocabulary makes most kids my age nervous. I liked that words made them uneasy and approved of Sheila's choices. My eyes drifted back to Jane. She'd pulled out car keys from her layers of clothing and dangled them in her thin fingers.

"Jane drives David to all his practices and to most of the games when the team doesn't take the bus. He's not allowed to drive since he failed a Breathalyzer last year. Jane is stuck chauffeuring around Candy and her friends sometimes, too. She really hates it."

"I bet she does."

My glance moved back to my mom and aunt. Mom motioned to her wrist, tapping her watch.

"Well, it looks like I've got to go. It was nice meeting you, Sheila."

"You, too, Zack. You're not like most hockey players, you know that?"

"Yeah, that's what they tell me."

"I'll see you at school," she said. "MSN message rooms have been lighting up with Zack spottings. You're going to get swarmed. I can help you find your way around if you want. I'll look for you."

I nodded, pushing myself away from the counter and walking away from Sheila. I pitched my half-empty Coke into the trashcan as I approached David with his sister and the other three girls.

"See you around, David." I turned to his sister. "Jane, you drive safely, now. He's an important hockey player." I winked at her.

She made a face at me. It wasn't a nice face.

I saw my mom and aunt watching. They both appeared a little startled by her expression.

I picked up my hockey bag. "Come on. Let's go."

My mom and aunt followed behind me.

As we strode through the parking lot, my mom hurried to catch up to me. "Who was the unpleasant girl with the serious fashion issues?" she asked. Mom wasn't exactly following the fashion police rules for women her age; she dressed in jeans and form-fitting t-shirts. She looked good, but different from most of the other moms—who usually wore sweater sets or velour track suits with pastel shirts.

"I don't know," my aunt interrupted. "I kind of liked her look."

For once I was happy about her desire to be involved in every conversation my mom and I had.

"I would be gothic and mysterious if I were sixteen." Aunt Diane gestured down to her Levi's jeans and plaid shirt, topped with a down vest. I smiled, thinking of the lesbian comment.

"I think I would wear really short skirts to show off my youthful legs," my mom said. "All I ever wore when I was a teenager were pants and jeans. God, Diane, remember when we didn't have any worries about cellulite, even though we lived on French fries with gravy?"

I tuned them out as they dove into a conversation about their long-lost youth, speedy metabolism, and great legs. My mom handed over the car keys, knowing I'd take every opportunity I could to practice driving. I clicked the car doors open using the remote, and held the back door for my aunt. My mother scooted around to the other side to hop in the passenger seat beside me.

Across the parking lot, Jane climbed into the driver's seat of a Pathfinder, while the other three girls giggled around her and David got into the passenger seat.

I didn't know why, but something about Jane intrigued me. Chances were she was smart. I liked that. She was also good-looking, but obviously not caught up in her looks. She actually tried to disguise them. She was the total opposite of Claire. Proper, conservative Claire, who, as Sheila helpfully pointed out, broke my heart.

Jane was the anti-Claire. And I was definitely interested.

CHAPTER 2

Haletown, Montana, wasn't so different from Kirkdale. Same stuff, different faces. People stared at me the first day of school. I ignored it. After that, life at Jefferson High turned out to be pretty much like life at most of the other schools I'd gone to. There were cool kids and kids who were not. Sometimes it's a question of what a guy considered cool. A few weeks in, and I'd already figured out who belonged to which groups. The Haves and the Have Nots. There were Jocks, and the kids who dated them. The Heads smoked pot in the bathrooms and on school grounds. The Arts were drama or rock and roll wannabes. Then there were the token Freaks and Losers, and a whole lot of people in the middle somewhere, all trying to fit in. Like Jane and Cassandra, her literary friend.

I drifted on the edges of acceptability. No one had any bones to pick with me. The Jocks acknowledged me without getting too chummy. The Heads and the Arts left me alone, probably because of my size. And I preferred it that way. No allegiance to anyone. A lone wolf.

By mid-October, the Huskies were on a losing streak. I tried to care, but for the first time in my life, it was hard to work up the energy. I just wasn't motivated. Mac showed zero interest in us playing like a team. The other guys were afraid of him and wasted time trying to make Mac shine. I didn't have the patience to show them what we were capable of when Mac wasn't spouting off and hogging the puck. So other than certain girls in the crowd, hockey actually kind of sucked. I lacked my usual drive to be the best, to win, and to stand out. I knew I wasn't playing with any sort of passion, but I really couldn't pinpoint exactly why or what I could do about it. Mom, on the other hand, worried about it often and none too quietly.

On this day at school, I navigated crowded hallways, trying not to be too obvious as I checked out Jane at her locker during the mad rush to change classes.

"Ouch! Hey, Superstud, watch where you're going."

I screeched to a halt and stumbled, trying not to bowl over Sheila. People swarmed around us, voices buzzing in the air. The rush was on, with students heading to lockers, classrooms, or off to a free period. Everyone was in a hurry.

Sheila planted herself in front of me, clutching her books to her chest the way she always did, as if she were trying to cover the size of her boobs. She looked at me with the patronizing, yet sympathetic expression she seemed to favor whenever she talked to me. Which was a lot these days. We'd become buddies. Friends, even.

"Sorry, Sheila. I wasn't paying attention to where I was going." I glanced at Jane's locker, then quickly back at Sheila.

"I noticed. You're staring at your girlfriend again." Sheila blatantly moved her eyes to where I'd been staring.

Trust Sheila to notice I'd been focusing on Jane, who leaned against her locker talking to her best friend, an overweight but flamboyant girl wearing a long dress with colorful scarves draped around her neck. Her short spiked hair must have kept at least one gel company in business.

"I don't know why you didn't fall in love with me instead," Sheila said. "God knows it would have made your life a lot easier."

I turned my attention to her and opened my mouth to speak.

"No. Stop. Don't humiliate me with an actual answer," she said, rolling her eyes. "I was kidding, anyway. I know, I know. We're friends. My charms are lost on you."

I grinned, glancing for a moment at Sheila's books blocking her abundant chest.

"Your charms are so not lost on me, Sheila," I teased. Who was I, not to notice her assets?

She smacked my arm with her hand.

"No, really, I was talking about your unique personality." I laughed.

"You're lucky I decided to be your friend at all." She squeezed her books again and glared at me.

"I didn't have much choice, did I?" I grinned. "Don't worry. I'm just kidding. You're da man."

The truth was, in the almost two months I'd been at school, she was my only real friend, besides some of the hockey players on my team. And those male friendships were superficial at best. The guys didn't know how to take me. I was one of them, but not really one of them. It was always the same everywhere I went.

Somehow, Sheila had figured out my secret and she was okay with me being a little odd. How could I not be? I've been hanging out with my mom and moving a lot for most of my life. Sheila sensed I didn't fit in, using the radar we misfits seem to have for each other. She'd apparently decided to take me on, maybe as a project or something.

"You know, Zack, since I'm probably the only virgin in this whole school, you're better off chasing other girls anyways." She smiled to show she joked about me loving her. But she didn't appear to be joking about the virginity part.

I didn't bother telling her she was wrong, and as a matter of fact, I was a virgin, too. But what Sheila didn't know wouldn't hurt her.

How I ended up a virgin at my age, me, a decent looking hockey player with plenty of opportunity, was mostly due to a cruel twist of fate named Claire. In ninth grade, I gave my heart to Claire. And she didn't go all the way. I didn't mind. I mean, I wasn't wild about waiting for her, but I waited. I thought I loved her, and I didn't want to make her do something she'd regret. And she seemed to be getting closer . . . .

Then, after denying me for almost two years, when she found out I was moving, she got really drunk at my going-away party. She disappeared, and when I finally found her, she was in the bushes going at it with another guy.

For the first time since I'd known her, Claire went past second base. Too bad it wasn't with me. Instead, she experimented with Neil, a guy on my hockey team. After I found them together, I just took off. On my way out, I turned back and saw her puking her guts all over the same bushes. Neil appeared to have vanished.

I'd almost gone to her. But in the end, I didn't.

After that, it was pretty clear we were over. I mean, what do you say after that? She didn't even try to call me.

From what I heard, she tried dating Neil for a few weeks, but it didn't work out. I could have saved her the grief. Neil wasn't renowned for his ability to be with only one girl at a time. I was almost more pissed at him. Claire was acting really immature, but he was just an asshole.

It's one of the reasons Sheila slipped so easily into the role of best friend. She'd never steal my girlfriend.

I shook off thoughts of Claire and turned my attention back to Sheila.

"Hey, what's this virgin thing? What about David Parker?" I still remembered what David had said the night I met Sheila.

"Oh, God." Sheila's face changed color and she looked around the hallway, which was quickly thinning out as people dashed to class. "I never really slept with him. I know he's told people, but I didn't know he'd said that to you. Anyhow, he was like, so drunk, he doesn't even remember what happened. All I did was take him home. Maybe we kissed a little, but man, I'm not that desperate or anything. Anyhow, I don't mind. It makes me sound more exciting."

"You think it sounds exciting? I think you're crushing." I'd seen her looking at David when she didn't know I was watching.

"You're the one with the crush." She peeked over at Jane, who had pushed away from her locker. "Not me."

I followed her gaze. Jane didn't know we were watching. Her head was thrown back, laughing. Her feminine, soft-looking neck was visible because she'd pulled her dark hair into a ponytail. With her hair off her face, the scowl replaced with a smile, she was really cute.

She turned her head slightly and then her eyes met mine. Suddenly she stopped smiling. Across the hallway, she stared at me for a second, emotionless, and not quite frowning. Then she lowered her gaze to her feet. My stomach performed a tribal dance.

"Damn," I said out loud.

Sheila started to laugh.

"I can't believe you're falling for her."

"I'm not."

She laughed some more. "Sure, Zack. Whatever you say. You know she'll never go out with someone like you."

I shrugged. The truth was, I couldn't stop thinking about Jane, and I saw her at practice almost every day. No matter when we were in the rink, she was almost always there, sitting in the warmest part of the arena, sipping hot chocolate and reading her books. Every once in a while I'd look up from a scrimmage, and then I'd catch her watching with those amazing, dark-rimmed eyes. For some reason, without even talking to me, she'd managed to get under my skin.

I started walking again.

"You going to Mac's Halloween party?" Sheila asked.

I shrugged. Mac, otherwise known as Trevor MacDonald, announced at practice last week that he was throwing a Halloween party.

"You might want to dress up as a captain," he said to me. "It's a dress-up party, after all. You may as well act out your fantasy."

The other guys laughed nervously, but I'd just smiled. He'd obviously heard rumors about our coach talking to me about taking over as captain. The coach wasn't too pleased with the team's losing streak, or with Mac's total lack of leadership.

I turned the coach down. I wasn't really into it. I didn't need the "C" on my chest to know I was a better player. Plus, I didn't want the responsibility. Mac didn't seem to need the extra hassle of having his leadership tested, either. My mom frothed a little when I told her. She wanted me to go for it, forget about Mac's ego or the fact that his dad was a crazed maniac. Sometimes, actually most of the time, my mom is way more competitive than I am.

We agreed to disagree. She wants so badly for me to make it as a hockey player at almost any cost. It's because of my dad—as if she can somehow bring back a part of him if I follow down his golden career path. Like I'd ever aspire to be like "dear old dad."

Mac had been playing with the Huskies all through high school, and he'd been captain every year. Far as I could tell, he was the product of the kind of father who made headlines in local papers. And I don't mean good headlines, either. His dad yelled at referees and called the opposition swear words from the stands. Very embarrassing. He timed shifts and came down on the coach if Mac wasn't getting enough ice time. Even though Mac was an asshole, I could relate to living in a father's shadow.

I wrote off most of his dorky behavior because of his dad. Of course, his dad hated me, too. And my mom. Because we all knew I played better than Mac could ever hope to move on the ice.

"You listening?" Sheila asked, bringing me back to the school hallway.

I glanced towards Jane's locker, but by now she was gone. I started walking to my next class. Sheila followed me, nipping at my heels like a puppy. A cute one, but kind of annoying.

"You know Jane will be there, right? At Mac's party?" Sheila pulled on an amber curl.

I watched the curl stretch out and then snap back to her head. I looked in her eyes to see if she was playing me.

"I'm totally serious. Here's the thing. The only way David can go to the party is if Jane drives him there and home. So I heard him begging her after practice. Candy's going, and he isn't going to let her loose at the party without him there to watch her. And for good reason, too. He was trying to bribe Jane."

Sheila's job at the arena had benefits. Eavesdropping, included.

I shrugged. "So she's going to go?"

Sheila smiled and nodded. She bounced up and down on her heels. I stopped. I'd reached my next class.

"So are you going?" Sheila asked.

"Are you?" I peeked into the classroom where I needed to be within seconds.

"Me?" She started to laugh. "You think they invited me?"

"They did if you come with me," I told her. "And, I just invited you."

She stared at me. "Kewl. A friend with privileges. So to speak. All right! I'll come with you. Somebody's got to keep you out of trouble. It's a dress-up party, you know."

I glanced back into the classroom. Kids were taking their seats, but Mrs. Smiley hadn't sat down yet.

"What are you going to dress as?" I asked Sheila.

"I don't know. Hey, I'm thinking, maybe Cupid. I have a morbid sense of humor." She laughed with her big baying laugh.

I shook my head and started walking into the classroom. "I gotta go, Sheila. I'll call you later," I said over my shoulder.

We both knew I was going to the party because I wanted to see Jane outside school or the hockey rink.

I walked down a narrow aisle of empty desks and sat in the middle of the classroom, beside a couple of girls who were like a pair of conjoined twins.

"That your girlfriend?" The more outgoing one asked as I sat.

I glanced at the doorway. "Sheila? No. We're friends."

"She slept with David Parker," her friend informed me.

I thought about dispelling the rumor, but remembered

Sheila thought it made her sound exciting. Who was I to take it away from her?

"That's the rumor," I said.

I opened my books and grinned at the pages in front of me.

I was definitely going to a Halloween party with my fellow virgin. Jane was going to be there, and so was I.

CHAPTER 3

On Halloween night I stood in front of the full-length mirror on the wall at the end of my bed and made faces at my reflection. I'd smudged my mom's eyeliner over my face to make beard stubble and a black eye. I tied a yellow bandana on my head, and for once, my scar worked to my advantage. I'd poked one of Mom's big gold hoop earrings into the empty hole in my left ear lobe.

"Argh," I mouthed to the mirror. "Me maties."

I got my ear pierced in seventh grade on a bet, although I didn't wear earrings anymore. I'm still not sure if Mom minded the pierced ear or not. All she said was that she wasn't the conservative one in the family—my dad was. Yeah. But he was also dead. When I showed her the earring, she told me my father would roll over in his grave.

Even now, I tried to imagine Jeremy Chase rolling over in his grave, but I couldn't picture his face. How could I? I shrugged, looking at my pirate self in the mirror and wondering what Jane would wear to a Halloween party.

I'd pulled on a torn-up old pair of jeans and a white

T-shirt with a pirate flag Mom had ironed on—her contribution to my costume.

She knocked on my door.

I turned and snarled. "Argh! What say you, scurvy dog?"

Mom never walks into my room without knocking. She respects my privacy as a "young man."

She opened the door, smiling when she spotted me. In her black yoga pants and white T-shirt, with her hair in a ponytail, she looked like she was about twenty. "You're the most gorgeous pirate I've ever seen."

She walked in and handed me a red silky scarf. "Here, use this for a sash." She tied it around my waist.

I checked in the mirror and nodded. "Cool."

Her eyes started to water up.

I turned. "Mom, please don't cry, and please don't get the video camera out."

"Sorry, Zachary." She wiped at her eye. "You just look so much like your dad right now."

Since I'd only been a couple of months old when the accident happened, I didn't have any memories about him. I'd seen photos and old footage of him playing hockey, and it was enough for me.

"I'm nothing like him," I snapped, and looked down.

"I know," she said softly. "So, you'll be at Mac's tonight?" she added, injecting false cheer to her voice. She didn't try to talk about dad much anymore. Which I saw as a good thing.

I nodded, glancing up.

"I'm glad you're making friends. Do you need a ride?"

"Sheila's picking me up."

Lucky for me, Sheila's already sixteen and the proud holder of a driver's license and owner of a beat-up old Honda she bought with her own money from working at the rink.

I couldn't wait to turn sixteen so I could get my own driver's license. I turned back to the mirror for a second, making another pirate-like face.

"Sheila's the redheaded girl who works at the arena?" she asked my reflection in the mirror.

I nodded.

"Is she your new girlfriend?" She struggled to keep her voice neutral.

"I already told you Mom, we're friends."

She nodded again, stepping forward to touch my cheek. "Okay. She doesn't seem like your type, that's all." She paused. "Do you miss Claire?"

Mom thought Claire was my type and probably thought I was still in love with her. Proper, well-dressed, conservative Claire. I never told Mom what Claire did. It would have devastated her more than it did me.

"I don't miss her. It's already been a long time." True. I didn't even think about her much anymore. My attention was focused on someone new. The anti-Claire.

She pursed her lips together. "Is this Sheila a nice girl?"

"She's my friend, Mom, so yes, she's a nice girl. Why don't you talk to her more and find out for yourself?"

"Yes, I should." She flicked her bangs out of her eyes.

"At least she has a job, unlike that dark, depressing girl I see reading in the stands all the time. David Parker's twin. She's always at the arena, always with a book. It's odd. Doesn't she have anything better to do?"

I glared at her. "You read all the time. So do I. Besides, Jane has to be there," I snapped. "David's parents work all the time. David can't drive because he lost his license, drinking. Jane has to take him. She doesn't like hockey much."

"I noticed," my mom said dismissively, as if such a notion made anyone untrustworthy.

"You don't know her."

She gazed into my eyes trying to read the thoughts in my head.

"No. I guess I don't." She touched my cheek again. "It doesn't matter, does it? Have fun tonight, Zachary. If you have too much to drink, or if Sheila isn't able to drive you home, you call, right? Aunt Diane is bringing over a movie, so I'll be home all night if you need me."

"I know, Mom." From the time I started going to co-ed parties, it was always the same story. She worried about drunk driving. And with good reason.

"I'm not planning on drinking too much, and Sheila is a responsible role-model teenager."

Mom never avoided talking to me about anything. Drinking. Drugs. The lectures started early. I guess they even sank in most of the time.

"Okay. Just be careful." She turned to leave my room. "Maybe you'll meet a nice girl tonight?"

I didn't answer. Obviously the one girl on my mind wasn't the one my mother pictured me with. Not that dark depressing girl who read books at hockey games.

A few minutes later, the front doorbell rang and I jumped down the stairs two at a time.

"I'll get it."

Aunt Diane was sitting in the big lounge chair in the living room. Mom sat on the couch. The two of them worked together at the store all day, but they still hung out together at night. It was kind of nice, but kind of sad at the same time. When Mom was a sales rep she always worked late, and she was usually too tired to socialize much. Instead, all she seemed to do was run and read.

She'd gone on a few dates over the years, but I never met any of the guys. Now back in her hometown working in retail, she had more free time and seemed happier, and a lot less stressed. I wondered if she would meet someone in Haletown. It might be nice for her. Weird. But nice.

"Zachary. You big handsome pirate," Aunt Diane called out, breaking into my thoughts. "How are you, sweetie?"

I smiled at her, as I headed down the hallway to answer the door. "Great, Aunt Diane. How's it going with you?"

I didn't wait for her reply but went right to the front door. I pulled it open and promptly started to laugh.

Sheila's face was painted black. She wore black tights and a black skullcap she'd tucked all her hair into. A circular black cardboard disk surrounded her.

"You're a hockey puck!" I said.

She beamed at me as I laughed, pleased that I got her joke. I'd told her what we called the hockey groupies in Kirkdale: "Pucks." I opened the door a little wider.

"Come on in, Puck."

My mom and aunt got up and followed me into the hallway. They watched Sheila turn sideways to fit through the door.

"How are you going to drive in that thing?" I asked.

"Oh, I take it off. I just wanted you to see the full effect." She smiled proudly.

"It's great," I told her.

My mom crept up behind us. "Mom, you know Sheila."

"Hi, Sheila. Cute costume!"

"Hi. Thanks! Well, it is a hockey party," Sheila said, glancing to me for help. She wasn't sure if my mom knew what Puck meant or not.

"I love it!" my aunt shrieked as she followed my mom into the hallway. "It's very clever."

"You have no idea," I mumbled under my breath.

My two-woman cheering section planted themselves in the hallway. Their faces were as eager as if they were coming with us.

"Have fun watching your movie," I said. Now please go away, I thought.

"What are you watching?" Sheila asked, with a little bit of hero worship in her eyes. A lot of kids looked at Mom that way sometimes, between her looks and her clothes. Even I know she's amazingly beautiful.

"*Sex and the City*, Season 6," Aunt Diane said.

"Yuck." I groaned.

"Wow." Sheila sounded impressed.

"Come on, Sheila." I hurried forward, pushing Sheila out. "And before you even begin to launch into an explanation of why you are watching that stupid show, we're out of here."

"Drive safely," my mom called to Sheila.

"Precious cargo, I know. Don't worry, Mrs. Chase." Sheila grinned as I gave her another push on her shoulder.

"You kids need a ride home, you call, okay?"

I closed the door behind me.

"God. How embarrassing," I said to Sheila as we headed towards her half-white, half-rust car. I only half meant it.

"No, they're very cool. And they're both so pretty. God, I can't believe your mom actually, like, acknowledges drinking. My mom's philosophy is 'don't ask, don't tell.' I'm not sure if she thinks I'm innocent or completely corrupt. At any rate, I haven't been able to stomach alcohol since the night I got drunk and threw up for two days after. I told my mom it was food poisoning."

I wasn't sure what to say. Her mother sounded scary. My mom didn't beat around the bush. She worried—because of my dad.

"Your mom is so young looking. I can't believe she's actually watching *Sex and the City*. My mom wanted to have the show censored and banned." She started to climb out of her hockey puck costume. She stepped out of the cardboard, opened the back door and lay it in the back seat.

"She's okay." I stared at Sheila in her black tights.

"Hey, you look hot." And she did. Her figure was not the typical teenage stick figure. With her hips and boobs, she looked fantastic.

"I'm a beluga whale."

I whistled. "No way, Hannigan. Under the skullcap and black paint, you're smoking. A delicious looking hockey puck. Better keep your costume on at the party if you want to get out of there still a virgin."

"You're delusional, Zack." She flashed a shy grin as she slipped into the driver's seat. "But thanks."

I crawled into the passenger seat. As I put on my seatbelt, I asked her, "Which guy are you so interested in, anyway?"

I watched her blush to a cute reddish shade. "Not interested in hockey players, Zack. They're Neanderthals."

"And that would make me . . . ?"

"An aberration." She turned on the engine and it sputtered to life.

"Aberration?"

"A peculiarity. Not the norm." She shoulder checked and pulled away from the curb.

"I know what it means, but why do you?"

"Same as you. I'm a geek. You're so not a hockey dude. You read. You're smart. I mean, when's the last time you got drunk and peed on someone's front lawn. Or had sex with more than one girl in one night. I'm sorry, my friend, but you are just too nice to be one of the hockey-team boys." She kept looking from me to the road.

"Hm." I didn't answer her accusation. I wasn't sure I liked being called a nice guy. I mean, I'd done my share of tormenting kids when I was younger. I'd pulled the legs off spiders and stepped on ants. I dated a girl because of her big boobs in seventh grade. I'd just wanted to touch them.

Along the way, I'd learned it was easier to blend in instead of trying to stand out. I stayed away from drinking too much because of what it did to my family. It had made it even smaller—by one.

I wasn't sure I liked the way Sheila viewed all hockey players, though. It was okay for me to be judgmental of the guys, since I was one of them. But she wasn't.

"You're the one with a job at the rink. And why are you so eager to hang out with the so-called Neanderthals?" I raised my eyebrows. "David Parker?"

Her face tightened up and she stayed focused on the road. It was surprisingly quiet on the roads for Friday night. "I like the game, not the players. Besides I'm only coming to the party because you asked me to. As a friend."

"Mm hm. Whatever you say."

Her face nearly vaporized with the steam that came off it.

"I told you I didn't really sleep with him."

Her squinting, angry eyes made me laugh. "No way, Hannigan. You're in love with David Parker, even though he torched your reputation and dates girls with single-digit IQs?"

She narrowed her eyes even more and didn't turn to face me. "I am not in love with David Parker," she said, through stiff, frowning lips.

I watched her for a moment, then I laughed again.

Yeah. And I wasn't in love with his twin sister. What a pair we were.

After we finally found a parking spot, I followed Sheila to the front door of the MacDonalds' mini-mansion. Mac's dad was obviously paid well for whatever it was that he did for a living. The bass from ear-splitting music buzzed from inside the house. Sheila opened the front door and my ears were filled with a rap song, kids' laughter, and several loud-mouthed voices. The air inside the house was hot, like the inside of a sauna. I smelled beer and sweaty bodies.

The front hallway was packed with kids, most of them in costumes. To the left of the front entrance was a dining room where the speakers were set up. It was packed with girls wearing tiny, revealing costumes, all standing in groups and moving their bodies in time with the loud music. Some girls were already paired up with guys, sitting on their laps. Sheila and I squeezed down the short hallway, and I high-fived a drunken kid from school who stuck out his hand like we were best buddies.

Kids were draped all over the stairs and the hallway leading to the kitchen and living room. The hall was open and spacious, but with so many bodies crammed into it, it was hard to move around. The music got a little quieter as we headed down the hall, but loud voices made up for it.

Sheila moved her head, indicating for me to follow her. She led us to the kitchen. I passed a couple of my teammates, disappointed to see a couple of other pirates among them. I exchanged handshakes and head nods as I passed the other guys. Most of them already had a girl draped on them. I knew from locker-room talk that not many had a regular girlfriend. But at the party, they managed to attract some good-looking arm candy.

Once we were inside the kitchen, also stuffed with bodies, Sheila led me to a table in the middle of the room. It was covered with a ripped black tablecloth that was soaked and soggy looking. White plastic cups were scattered around the table, and in the middle of it was a deep punch bowl. In the liquid we could see pieces of something eyeballish floating. I hoped they were little green grapes and nothing worse.

The mayhem in the kitchen bled into the living room area. Kids filled most of the available space, all of them standing or sitting on the furniture and floors.

Sheila leaned over and yelled in my ear. "Have some of that punch; some kids think that Mac's dad actually makes it for him, but nobody knows for sure. It's pretty powerful, though, so take it easy and don't say I didn't warn you."

I nodded. I helped myself to a cup and dipped it into the punch, filling the cup. I took a sip and winced. It was heavy on vodka, and a little light on fruit juice.

"You mean Mac's dad knows about the alcohol?" I asked almost shouting to be heard.

Sheila shrugged. "Not technically. But who's going to say anything?" She glanced around the room. "He's not anywhere around at these parties. Not visibly anyhow. But

I'm sure he's watching from somewhere. No one gets too out of hand at Mac's parties. They save that for other people's houses."

I shrugged and took another sip of my drink, looking around the room at the scene. That's when I spotted her. Jane.

She sat in the middle of the living room, blending into the black sectional couch. She seemed oblivious to the party going on around her. She wore her usual baggy black clothes. No Halloween costume for Jane. A guy dressed as Batman sat down on the couch across from her with a girl in a French maid costume on his lap. They were doing some heavy Frenching. Jane turned her body away from them and blocked them from view with her book. I smiled and took another sip of my drink. She looked like a little girl who stumbled upon an adult dress-up party, with no way to escape except into her book.

"Go get her, Tiger." Sheila gave me a little push on my shoulder.

I dug my feet into the ground and gave Sheila a dirty look. "Bite me, Hannigan."

"With pleasure." She pushed me harder towards Jane.

I took another sip of the horrible punch and took a couple of tentative steps towards Jane, wondering what I could say that wouldn't sound lame. A warm body pressed up close to mine, interrupting my thoughts.

"Hi, Zack Attack. I'm Mona," a slurry and wet voice said into my ear.

I glanced down at the tasty creature who'd attached herself to my right side, her lean legs pressed up against my thigh. I could feel her boobs squishing into my bicep. She wore a tiny bathing suit top filled past capacity, and a grass skirt barely covering her bathing suit bottom. Around her neck was a plastic yellow lei. She was one of the girls who hung with David's girlfriend at the rink sometimes.

"Hey, Mona, how's it going?"

She'd never said much to me before. I'd always thought she was a litte shy, despite her reputation.

"Want to get lei'd?" she stood on her tiptoes, and purred into my ear. She wobbled, picking up her lei and rubbing it between her fingers, and then she stuck it between her lips and sucked on it seductively.

I looked into her eyes to confirm what I suspected. Her eyes were shining, glassy, and red. I smelled alcohol fumes on her breath. She was loaded.

"You're having a good time?" I said, like an idiot.

"I'm Mona," she said again, saying her name as if it were Moan-a. Very MTV. I wondered if she was sixteen yet. I didn't wonder if she was a virgin. She was pretty out of it.

She giggled and put her arms around my neck. She leaned forward. "You're so cute. I adore you."

I turned my head to avoid sucking face with her, despite the screams of every inch of my body. I peeled her arms off my neck.

"Mona. You're a goddess, trust me. Don't think I don't appreciate the attention. God, I do. But the thing is, I kind of came here to talk to someone. Can you let me by?"

Her mouth dropped open. Her eyes flashed. "You don't know what you're missing," she slurred.

She stumbled a little. I reached out my free hand to steady her, and she collapsed into my arm, giggling and staring up at me, pulling me close to her face.

"I give the best BJs in Jefferson High," she confided in a loud whisper. Her breath smelled like a dropped bottle of booze smashed on the kitchen floor.

"I'm sure you do," I said, wishing for a moment I'd never laid eyes on Jane Parker.

"Do you want to find out?" she whispered.

Yes. There was movement in the nether regions. I'm a teenager. My hormones tend to rage.

"Whoa, Mona. I think you need to chill." I shook her off my arm. I leaned down to remove her while I still had some control.

She giggled again, and as I opened my mouth to say something more, she kissed me. She slid her tongue into my mouth, and moved it around in a most seductive and promising way. God. It had been awhile.

I wanted to resist, I really did, but man, she was so sexy and willing and all the things I hadn't experienced in so long. I wanted to just bury myself inside her. I put my hand on her sexy, firm waist and her scrumptious soft body pressed against mine. Good sense flew out. I gave in. I kissed her back, deeply, like I meant it. Because for that exquisite moment, I really, really did. I wanted her. An easy thing for the virginal Zack Chase. Jane didn't even like me anyways. Mona, well, she did.

I pushed her against the wall and she jutted her hips against mine. She reached down and actually grabbed me, you know, there. I groaned. It felt so good. I needed this.

I did. All the old frustration from Claire resurfaced. Claire who did it with some other guy the minute she found out about me moving away.

Jane. She meant work. A lot. Not Mona. Mona was a sure thing. I needed that. Badly.

"Let's find a room," she moaned into my ear.

I groaned again and kissed her deeper. I reached down, wanting to touch her everywhere, wanting to let her take me where I'd never been before. Away. And then she did it.

She hiccupped. Not a little demure lady-like sound, but a gross, wet, "oh my God I'm going to throw up" moment. Her hand clamped over her mouth with sheer force; I stepped back and straightened up.

She made a horrible retching sound again and her body kind of heaved. She panted with her hand over her mouth. She closed her eyes, swallowing and mumbling to herself.

As I watched her trying not to spew, my brain began unfuzzing from hormonal overload. I realized what the hell I'd just done.

My eyes immediately shot to the couch. There was no one there. Jane was gone.

CHAPTER

4

I scanned the living room, but Jane had disappeared.

Great. Mona, meanwhile, seemed to find her mojo again. Her hand left her mouth and a gleam came back into her eyes. She giggled.

"Come on. Let's go find a room." Mona pulled on my arm, staggering a little as she tried to tug me towards the stairs. "Can you get me a drinkie first?"

I pushed her back gently, then dragged my hands through my hair. "God, Mona. You don't need another drinkie. I'm an asshole and you're completely wasted. You need to go home before someone takes advantage of you."

Someone like me. Damn. What the hell was wrong with me? I looked around to see if there was a friend of hers nearby, but no one paid attention to her. Even Sheila had disappeared. Thank God. I prayed she hadn't witnessed what I'd just done. I was an asshole.

I stepped away from Mona, ignoring her drunken fuss behind me, as she sputtered and stumbled around.

I walked out of the kitchen, sipping my drink for

courage, and searching around the house for Jane. I wondered how much she'd seen, and how I was going to get her to forgive me. I didn't spot her in the sea of bodies in the hallway or in the foyer. I squeezed by Sheila in the hallway, as she talked to one of the defensemen wearing a Ninja outfit. Her arms waved animatedly in front of her. I guessed she was giving him tips on how to improve his game. If he was sober enough to listen, she could probably help. The girl could talk serious hockey.

I spotted David in the dining room. He was wearing a tight pair of jeans that made my private parts wince. Thick gold chains wound around his neck like pet snakes and he chewed an unlit cigar.

I guessed he was supposed to be a pimp or a gigolo in that outfit. Candy danced around him in a tight wispy dress that reminded me of something a genie would wear. Her eyes were closed, her head back, her long blonde hair swaying across her back. She ran her fingers through her hair and along her sides, tracing her curves seductively while David howled like a werewolf. It looked like she was seconds away from an orgasm of self-love.

David turned his back to me and I smiled when I read his shirt. In large white letters it spelled out TEAM STALLION.

A shirt to make his mama proud.

I bolted two by two up the stairs and scanned the room below. Still no sign of Jane. I continued up the stairs, squeezing past bodies draped over the railings. By the time I reached the top, I decided it would be a good time to find a bathroom. I spotted a closed door down the surprisingly empty hallway.

I hurried towards it and reached out to jiggle the knob, hoping it was the bathroom. I heard angry voices on the other side of the door and stopped turning. Great, a couple having a fight. The usual teenage drama at drinking parties.

"Shit." I said under my breath.

I stood in front of the door weighing my options, moving back and forth from one leg to the other and trying not to think about how badly I now needed to pee.

It was no use. I needed to pee. Badly.

I knocked on the door again. I heard a yelp, then some scuffling, followed by a deep voice: "Go screw yourself, we're busy in here."

I recognized Mac's voice. With one of his groupies?

"Hey, man. It's Zack. I really need to pee." I banged on the door for emphasis.

"Zachary?" A small voice in the bathroom called my name. "Zachary. Let me out."

"Jane?" I stared at the door, puzzled.

I heard low voices and then angry swearing. Mac.

"Get the hell out of here, man. This is none of your business."

Definitely Mac. "Open the door." My entire body tensed. My free hand formed into a tight fist. I bent and put my drink on the floor and stood, ready to break the door down with my bare hands.

"This is personal. Beat it."

"Open the door, Mac. I mean it." I pounded it with my fist for good measure.

"Chase. Beat it. This is none of your business."

"Zachary, you jerk, open the door." Jane sounded closer to hysterics.

I banged on the door with both of my fists. "Open the freaking door, Mac, or I'll open it for you." I shoved my shoulder against it with everything I had. It hurt, but it didn't budge the door.

I was about to crash into it again when I heard another commotion—and then the door opened. Mac's face was a mask of anger. His eyes were slits, his face even more sinister with the red he'd painted on to go with his red pants and shirt. A devil costume.

Jane shrieked in anger as she ran out with her head lowered. She bolted down the hallway and down the stairs.

I stared at Mac. "What the hell were you doing to her?"

"It's none of your business. Stay out of this. It doesn't concern you. Say anything to anyone and I'll kick your ass." He stepped out of the bathroom.

"With whose foot?" I thrust my shoulders back so I appeared bigger. I had an inch or so on Mac, but he had about fifteen pounds on me.

I was mad enough to give him a good fight though. I wanted to find Jane and make sure she was okay, but I needed to deal with this asshole first.

He took a step towards me. We stared into each other's eyes. I glared at his tiny slits and my breathing accelerated. My body was in attack mode. I reached my hand out and pushed his chest. Hard.

"You leave Jane alone," I barked.

His eyes narrowed even more. "What's it to you? You freak."

I ignored him and he smiled. It was the coldest smile I'd ever seen. "Touch me and you'll never play hockey in this town again."

If I hadn't been so pissed, I would have laughed.

"What the hell does this have to do with hockey, Mac?" I spit out his name like it was a dirty word. "Leave Jane alone, or I will make you very, very sorry."

He pushed on my chest and my adrenaline raced.

"Who the hell do you think you are? Jane's protector? And this has everything to do with hockey, trust me. You're new around here. You don't know anything. That chick doesn't deserve to be protected or fought over. Just so you know, she was about to blow me. She's a bitch who likes rough foreplay. It turns her on."

I sucked in a breath. I glanced over my shoulder towards where Jane disappeared. I shook my head. Her voice, the way she scurried off. Definitely not foreplay.

Mac took advantage of the moment. He grabbed me and pulled me into a headlock. I struggled to get free but he held me down.

I heard male laughter behind us.

"Whatsamatter, Zack Attack? You trying to tackle the captain 'C' off Mac?"

David. With my head upside down, I made out a liquor-enhanced, inverted smile.

Eddie and Cole, Mac's best buddies, lined up behind him. Mac breathed into my ear. "Say a word about Jane to Parker, and you're dead meat." To the guys he called, "Why would he even try for captain, when I am so clearly the man?"

In my ear: "You're a loser. A nothing. The only reason you're on my team is because your dad was a big deal and the coach liked the idea of your name. Too bad your daddy liked whores and got so drunk with them that he killed himself."

He threw me down to the ground. I stumbled and righted myself. David and the guys were watching with amusement.

"Testosterone is such an interesting chemical," said a voice from behind them.

Sheila took up the width of the entire hall behind them in her hockey puck costume.

I ignored the audience, leaning forward so only Mac could clearly hear every word I said.

"My dad is none of your business, Mac. And for your information, if I wanted the precious captain 'C' on my uniform, I'd have taken it. It was already offered to me. I said no as a favor—to you. So push me again and I'll take it. Oh, and touch Jane again, and I'll make you sorry you were ever born."

I turned back to the guys and Sheila. "Mac was just explaining why his daddy likes to hold drinking parties for underage kids."

The faces of my fellow hockey players shifted, except for David's. He was too drunk to feel tension. He whooped it up, laughing and slapping at his leg. "Zack's attacking Mac."

"David. Go and find your sister. Right now." I ordered. "She needs to go home." I looked pointedly at Mac.

David's smile faded and confusion clouded his

features for a moment. He looked around the hallway as if searching for Jane. "Where's the she-devil? Is she okay?" His voice wobbled.

Mac stepped closer to the boys. "Hey. David and I were talking the other day about how your mom likes to have sex with the ladies. Maybe that's why your dad drank so much? Maybe that's why he picked up women when he was on the road? Trying to deal with the fact he married a lesbian?" Mac's voice was cold and low. The air in the hallway seemed to grow still.

My muscles went rigid. I saw nothing except Mac's sinister face. I wanted to punch it more than I'd ever wanted to hurt someone in my life.

"I'm going to be sick." Sheila pushed past the guys, grabbed my arm and made some loud, rude choking noises. The guys, even Mac, all automatically moved back.

"Take your groupie slut and get the hell out of here," Mac called.

"Groupie?" Sheila stopped pulling on my arm and turned. "You moron, that's more insulting than slut."

She dragged me down the hallway, grumbling and swearing under her breath. When we started down the stairs she hissed, "You do not want to get into a fight with Mac at his own party, Zack. Let's get out of here."

She practically pushed me down the stairs. In her costume, she took up the entire hall behind me, so I couldn't even attempt to look back at Mac.

She chatted randomly to people we passed as she pushed me down the hallway through the party and towards the front door.

"Gotta go. See you all later. Nice costume, Tiffy. Great look for you, Sandy. You do French maid well. It's especially fetching." She continued to mumble and make comments as she pushed me along.

I stopped before we reached the door and she crashed into me. I turned.

"We have to find Jane before we go," I shouted over the music.

"Zack. Give it up. She's never going to crush on you. She really hates hockey players." She pushed at me, trying to get me out the door.

She didn't know how much worse I'd made it. Making out with Mona in the hallway like a dog in heat. Man, I'd really messed up. Still, I wasn't leaving without knowing she was okay.

"No. I'm serious. I'm not leaving without seeing her."

I wasn't going to tell Sheila about Mona or say anything about Mac and Jane in the bathroom. Far as I could tell, Jane deserved to hang on to her dignity. Me, well, I'd fend for myself.

Sheila rolled her eyes. "This party totally blows," she yelled. She leaned forward on her tippy toes and spoke in my ear. "I saw Jane head outside. Go see if she's still there. I have to pee. When I come back, we'll go."

She turned and waddled off in search of the bathroom on the main floor.

God, I needed to pee, too. Badly at this point. But I had to find Jane first, to make sure she was okay. My bladder threatened to explode, but I pushed my way out the front door. A vacuum of silence surrounded me when I stepped out into the night air and closed the door behind me. The cold fall air hit. I shivered and looked around. I spotted her.

"Jane?" I called softly. She stood at the end of the driveway, her back towards me.

She didn't turn to look at me. I hesitated for a second, then started walking towards her. She didn't move.

When I reached her I put my hand out to tap her shoulder, to let her know I was behind her. She pulled away.

"Go away." She didn't turn to look at me.

"Are you okay?" I didn't move.

Her shoulders went up and then slowly down, as if she'd inhaled a big breath of air.

"What happened?" I asked.

"I don't want to talk about it. Not with you, not with anyone." She spun around to glare at me, her eyes flashing. "Don't tell anyone what happened," she ordered.

Surprised, I shook my head. "I won't. I would never. But I mean, come on, Jane. It wasn't your fault. You can talk to me."

"Why? So you can broadcast the news to the guys in the locker room?"

I put my hands up in defense.

She checked out her feet and peered up again at me, her eyes unreadable. "Please don't say anything, Zachary."

I nodded, wishing I could find the words to make things right between us. "I'm on your side, just so you know. I'll kick his ass if he ever touches you again. He even blinks at you, you tell me, okay, Jane? I mean it; you tell me if he even breathes in your direction."

She didn't say anything, but her features softened a little. "You're a pirate," she said.

Her eyes were red and she'd wiped away all of her usual make-up.

"You're beautiful," I said, without thinking.

Her eyebrows crinkled, her forehead furrowed. She took a small step back from me. "Tell that to Mona, Romeo."

I shook my head, about to try to exonerate myself in some way and spout some romantic garbage to her when a voice bellowed out from the front door.

"Jane, Jane, you big fat pain," sang out a drunken voice.

I turned. David was wobbling at the front door, his face blurry and unfocused.

"Jane, Jane, you're ruining my fun again," he continued happily into the night air.

A breeze rippled my arm hair as Jane rushed past me towards her brother.

"David! You're being an asshole. Cut it out," she called, as she hurried towards him. She didn't sound mad, just resigned. "You're drunk and I need to get out of here. We're going. Are you taking Candy with you?"

"Candy, Candy, my sweet Candy," he bellowed back into the house.

"I'll go find her," Jane said.

I started walking towards them as Jane hurried past David, disappearing into the house.

David punched me on the arm when I reached him. "Hey, man. Come with us. Party at my place. Parents aren't home until late. Mona wants to hula you."

At the door, Sheila poked her head out from behind David.

"Shelly," David yelled happily to her face. "I think I love you." He grabbed her by the cardboard, pulled her in and kissed her on the cheek.

"Parker. You're drunk again," Sheila said.

"And you're jealous he's all mine," a smooth voice said from behind Sheila.

"Oh, Candy. You're so sweet," David sang in his off-key baritone voice. "Come to me, babe."

Candy pushed past Sheila's costume and gave her a withering glance as she passed. Candy slithered close to David, wrapping her arms around his waist and holding him like he was her trophy.

"Let's get out of here. This party is lame," Candy announced to those of us gathered on the front porch. "Costumes. God. How pathetic." She seemed to have forgotten she was dressed up.

"Yes. I'm so glad you came as yourself, Candy," Sheila said. "What are you, a hooker?"

David's laugh burst out like thunder. Candy hit him and shot Sheila a poisonous look. "Zack, come with us. Jane's driving us to David's place. Mona's coming, and I think she likes you." She wiggled her finger at me and winked, turning to block out Sheila. "Your hockey puck friend can drive herself home. She's used to leaving alone."

I glanced at Sheila, her face expressionless except for the tightness of her lips. Mona slipped out from behind her and stumbled on the front porch into the night air. She was lucky she was well lubricated with alcohol, considering the scanty amount of clothing she wore, otherwise she'd be freezing her almost exposed ass off. "Zacky, keep me warm." Mona stepped towards me, sliding her hands around my waist and untying my sash.

I tried to untangle her and get my sash back as Jane squeezed out onto the front stoop dangling car keys on her fingers. Her eyes narrowed when she saw Mona playing with my sash. When she looked at me, a chill ran down my back. She dismissed me, turning to her brother and his attached-at-the-waist girlfriend.

"David, bring your wench, we're going."

"Zacky's coming with us." Mona giggled, grabbing at my hands. I pulled away.

Sheila charged down the stairs, knocking into Mona as she tried to squeeze past. Sheila was furious, but somewhat slowed by the bulk of her costume.

"No, I'm not!" I said, at the exact same time that Jane growled, "No, he's not."

I grabbed Sheila by the arm, trying to keep her from taking off without me. "Sheila, wait. I'm coming with you."

"Don't do me any favors," she fumed, as she tried to shake me off.

"Zacky, I need a little company. Warm me up," Mona moaned on my other side, seemingly oblivious to everything but herself.

I brushed her off my arm. "Leave me alone, Mona," I snapped. My voice finally made an impact and she responded by stepping away, her eyes wide with disbelief.

I glanced at Jane. Ahead of us, on the driveway now, her arms crossed, her foot tapping up and down. At my side, Sheila grumbled and cursed as I held her arm.

"I'll see you around," I said directly to Jane. She looked right at me with her big pale eyes. For a moment the rest of the world faded as Jane and I stared at each other. Then she glanced at Mona, looked sort of disgustedly at me, and then pointedly looked away.

"Let me go." Sheila stomped on my foot, hard.

"Oww!" I said, glancing down at Sheila, but not letting go of her arm. Jane walked away, with David and Candy following unsteadily behind her, arm in arm. David sang a happy little tune, oblivious to the conflict hanging in the cool night air.

Mona stared at me. "Aren't you going to come?" she pouted.

When I shook my head no, she made a mewing sound, turned and fled, running and stumbling as she tried to catch up with Candy and David.

Sheila stopped squirming and I let go of her arm. "Did you think I was really going to leave with her?"

She shrugged.

"Give me a little credit, okay, Sheila?"

"I guess I keep forgetting that you're not like the other boys. I should have known." She mumbled under her breath.

"What?"

"That you have the hots for the bad girl and wouldn't ruin it for a fling with anyone else."

Too bad I already had. I sighed.

"Jane is not a bad girl."

Sheila giggled and pulled on my arm. "You didn't even deny it. You do love Jane, the weirdest girl in junior class."

I ignored her peels of laughter. I wanted to beat myself up for being so stupid with Mona. Then I thought about Jane's frightened voice from inside the bathroom. Mac was going to pay for scaring her, for trying to hurt her. He was also going to pay for what he'd said about my dad. How I felt about him was one thing. But a guy didn't call down another guy's dad. I ignored what was in my head and concentrated on the pain in my bladder.

"God. I have to pee so bad my teeth are floating," I growled.

I spotted a bush. "Wait there. I'll be right back."

I heard Sheila cracking up as I watered the MacDonalds' rose bushes. The least I could do for Trevor.

"Oh, Zack. You really *are* a hockey player," she yelled, sounding almost proud.

CHAPTER

It was time to make my move.

"Coach Cal. I need to talk to you," I called through my facemask.

The coach nodded, skating around me to keep his eye on the drills going on across the rink.

"Sure, Chase. Talk to me after practice, now get back in there."

"I want to talk to you about the captain position."

He stopped moving and stared at me. "What about it?"

"Is it still open?" I moved my feet back and forth on the ice.

Coach Cal glanced across the ice at Mac. He stood behind the goalie's net, his stick holding the puck still as he watched us.

"Not so much, son. We're well into the season now." He looked back at me, his face sober.

"I know. But I think I can do a better job. Maybe I could motivate the team. Shake things up." Coach Cal's eyes went back to Mac. He'd passed the puck to another player.

We were on a losing streak. The coach cocked his head. He lifted the whistle hanging around his neck to his lips. "Let me think about it, son." He blew the whistle and skated away from me, towards the scrimmaging players in front of the net.

I smiled as I watched him go. Thinking about it. A good start. My belly tingled with the power building inside. My hockey DNA. I gripped my stick hard. Time to start playing hockey like I'd been born to play it. I'd been slacking off, but in that instant, I knew I could get it back: ignite the "win" gene. A thrill raced through my entire body, like I'd just peeked at a girlie magazine in the grocery store. I felt more alive than I had in weeks.

"Oof."

Someone shoulder checked me hard from behind. I stumbled and then fell on my knees, completely caught off guard.

Mac sprayed ice in my face with his skates as he stopped right in front of me.

"What's the matter, Pretty Boy? Not used to a little one-on-one?"

"Back off, Mac," I growled and stood up on my skates. I used my extra couple of inches to my advantage and stared him down.

"You really need to get some practice time in, instead of spending your time sucking up to the coach. You act like a girl, the way you expect special treatment on the ice." He didn't move away from me.

I grinned, not letting him goad me. "And I think you need to work on your leadership skills, big guy. Talk around here is you're not living up to your captain status. You kind of blow as a leader. Never mind that you can't score a goal."

Sprinkle, sprinkle, sprinkle. I was planting some seeds. And in a way it was true. Sheila and I had been discussing his unworthiness as a captain just the other day. I knew most of the guys on the team agreed, but they were all too chicken to say anything.

Mac glared at me, his eyes slits under his clear plastic hockey visor. "Bullshit."

I shrugged.

I actually saw his left eye twitch. In a flash he threw down his stick, stepped forward, and shoved me with both hands. I let myself fall to the ground again, taking a bit of a dive.

Then I heard Coach Cal's whistle.

"Chase, MacDonald. Cut it out," he bellowed as he speed skated towards us.

I pushed myself up off the ice again.

"Mac. Go to the locker room and cool off. Chase—get the hell out of here. Get over to the scrimmage."

Mac started to protest.

"Zip it, Mac. Start acting like the captain of this team and not some stupid hothead."

I worked hard to keep myself from smiling. The seeds were planted in the ground. Fertilized, even.

I turned away from Mac and the coach as they argued back and forth. I glanced into the stands. Jane's head was up from her book. I caught her eye, and she immediately ducked her head back down and started reading again.

I grinned.

I saw Mac's dad rushing from the stands towards the glass. His face distorted with rage, he was already beginning to yell like a madman. My smile widened.

"What the hell is going on," he hollered at the coach.

I skated away from them towards the rest of the team scrimmaging by the net.

"What's up?" asked David when I skated towards him, ready to show them what I was really made of.

"Coach Cal says Mac's being a stupid hothead." I echoed the coach's very own words. I shrugged and skated into the action.

"Are you crazy, Zack?" Sheila hissed, jumping out from behind a corner as I emerged from the locker room.

It had been unnaturally quiet in the locker room before I'd left. Mac cleared out before I hit the changing room, where the bragging and kidding were low-key. The guys kept glancing sideways at me, as if I were going to self-combust or something. I wasn't sure if they were pissed at me or on my side. They sensed something big going down, maybe a changing of the guard? They didn't know yet who'd win, or even who deserved their support.

"Shouldn't you be working?" I asked Sheila as she grabbed my arm and pulled.

"I took a break." She frowned. "Mac's dad is fuming. What did you do to him out there?"

I just shrugged. I wasn't raised to be afraid of adults. Even irrational, scary ones like Mac's dad. Daddy wanted to take me on? Well, I was okay with that.

Luckily, there was comfort knowing I was an asset to my team. Of course, even if they rebelled and kicked me off for mutiny, I could always play hockey somewhere. Truth be told, I wasn't married to the Huskies and their no-shower, rancid locker room. Except Jane's brother played for them. Which forced Jane to be at all the games and practices. And I needed time to work on her after that Halloween party. There still was that. Hmm.

As soon as I rounded the corner, my mother rushed towards me. Her face was bright red, her eyes almost burning, a sure sign she was angry. People say my mom and I look alike. If it's true, every emotion I experience must be written all over my face. She's not exactly a poker face, my mom.

I stopped walking and straightened myself up to my full height as she hurried towards me.

"Zachary! Come on. Let's go. We're out of here." She almost bounced as she gestured with her hands, hurrying me along.

I glanced down at Sheila. She stared at both of us with big eyes.

"Hello, Mrs. Chase," she said in a shy, un-Sheila-like voice.

Mom glanced at her and gave her a quick dismissive smile.

"Hi, Sheryl. Don't mean to be rude, but we have to go. Now, Zachary!" Her attention was back on me. Her face was pulsing.

"Okay, Mom. I'm coming. Chill."

I sauntered behind her as she hurried towards the exit of the rink. She was like a horse at the gates, penned up and furious, needing to escape and run.

She glanced nervously around, then stopped walking and took a step back, putting out her hand to stop me from moving farther. That's when I saw him, too.

Mac's dad.

He strode across the lobby to reach us, practically running. I watched him approach, careful to look him straight in the eye. I couldn't help a nervous little grin though. I mean, it's a little intimidating to be the red flag with a fully grown bull charging me. Mac's dad looked like he wanted to string me up by my privates and leave me hanging until I was dead or at least incapable of manly acts. He hurried towards me with rage in his eyes.

"You," he shouted. "Boy. You wait right there."

My mom cursed. I stared at her, shocked. She never says bad words. Ever.

"Please act like a grown-up and leave my son alone," she said to the advancing madman. She took a step so she was right beside me.

"Let me handle this, Mom," I said. I planted my feet in the ground, stood a little straighter, and casually dropped my hockey bag to the floor. Sheila stepped up so she was on my right, beside my arm. Great. How tough could I look, flanked by a pair of short women?

"Who the hell do you think you are?" he demanded as he rushed towards me.

"I'm Zachary Chase, but the boys call me Zack

Attack," I answered, my nervous smile getting a little wider. I put out my hand to stop my mom from moving towards him. He looked like a pissed-off caged bear that was about to escape his confines to deliver payback for real or imagined wrongs. I didn't envy Mac, being on the end of this anger at home.

"Wipe the insolent smile off your face, boy, and show me some respect when I talk to you." Mac's dad was the kind of corporate shark you could spot a mile away. It was all about winning and demanding respect. His blondish hair was shaved close to his head. I imagined premature baldness. His thick neck matched a broad, thick body. Seasoned and fit, but he was still shorter than me.

Thankful for the slight height advantage, I sincerely hoped I wasn't actually going to need it. I stayed optimistic that Mac's dad wasn't about to take a round out of me in the middle of the hockey rink, in front of my mom. To her credit, she held her tongue.

I stared straight into his eyes, though, not backing down. I also didn't show the building anxiety that was making me a little jumpy. I was almost tempted to call him "sir," but I stopped myself. From what I'd seen and heard of Mr. MacDonald, he certainly didn't deserve it.

"I show respect to my elders when they earn it, Mr. MacDonald." Even I was surprised by how calm my voice sounded. I sensed my mom and Sheila staring at me like I'd turned into a blue-headed monster.

Behind Mac's dad, I saw some of my teammates moving closer to the action. No sign of Mac in the area yet, but I knew he'd be around soon. I glanced back at his dad's lethal eyes, now refocused on my mom.

"You raise this hippy kid in a barn, lady? Look at his hair. He looks like a girl." He scoffed.

To my mom's credit, she didn't flinch or fire back an insult. She stared him down with a look that would have sent me scurrying for cover. Mr. MacDonald didn't know what he was dealing with. He didn't want to piss off Mrs. Chase.

"I sure don't play like a girl, though, do I? *Sir*." I pronounced *sir* with what I hoped was irony. I glanced at Sheila and my mother. "No disrespect to these females at my side."

Out of the corner of my eye, I saw the unmistakable form of Jane, moving closer to the confrontation site. I didn't doubt all eyes were on us now. I really hoped not to embarrass myself.

"Please don't insult my son. Treat him like an adult. He's almost sixteen," my mom said through clenched teeth. Very clenched.

"Your son is a fairy-boy, ma'am. The only reason he's playing with the Huskies is because of your late husband. Whose reputation, by the way, explains some of this kid's wild behavior. He doesn't deserve to be on this hockey team."

That was it. My mother inhaled a sharp breath.

Calling me names and going after her late husband was one thing. Insulting my hockey skills was a whole other matter.

I jumped in. "Hey, keep my family out of this, Mr. MacDonald. God. It's just a game. Lighten up."

"If it's only a game to you, then you shouldn't be on

the team," Mr. MacDonald spit out and crossed his arms as he stared down me and my mom.

I took offense. "Whatever, dude. I like to win as much as the next guy." I turned away from him and picked up my hockey bag. Sheila moved in closer again, once the bag was on my shoulder. I wasn't going to stand around talking to this goon all day.

"I wouldn't know it from watching you play. You're lazy and you contribute nothing but animosity to this team." Mr. MacDonald's eyes flashed and he grinned the meanest smile I'd ever seen.

My mom actually growled in anger. I glanced down at her, a little concerned about that noise. She was practically foaming at the mouth, and she was about to defend her cub. I jumped in before she started yelling.

"Maybe it just looks that way because this whole team needs to be pushed. Maybe even with a new leader, *sir*." I used the same ironic tone. "Your son's an uninspiring bully and a terrible team captain." I heard a whoop of rage behind him, proof that Mac lurked. Now he charged forward, heading straight for me. I dropped my bag again, automatically stretching my arms out in front of Sheila and my mom, protectively.

My mom pushed my arm away and stepped in front of me. Oh good. Now my mom wanted to fight Mac.

Luckily, he stopped.

I gently moved my mom aside. Mac stood in place, his foot practically scratching at the ground, ready to charge me like a bull.

"I'm not going to fight in front of my mom," I told

him. "Matter of fact, I'm not going to fight you at all. You want to settle this, let's do this on the ice."

I stared into his dark eyes. "That a deal, Mac? Or are you all words, no action. Think you can show me up on the ice?"

Mac took the bait. "Penalty shots. Next practice."

I suppressed a smile. No problem. I shrugged and tried to look worried.

"Most goals out of ten shots. Pick your goalie," Mac said, looking pleased with himself.

"Forget it, Trevor." His father growled behind him. I heard uncertainty under the indignation. He was afraid I'd beat his son. He wasn't a stupid man. "You're not making deals with this punk. I want him off the team."

"He's the best player out there, hands down," my mom piped up. She wasn't going to let anyone berate my hockey skills. "Your boy afraid?"

Oh good. Now my mom was taunting them.

"He's a punk," Mac's father said. "Just like his father was."

Mom took a step towards him. My tiny little waif of a mother, taking on an angry burly man. No, I don't think so.

"Mom." I pulled her arm.

She shushed me. "Zachary's father is not your business. Zachary is not leaving this team just because you feel threatened by him."

Mac's dad shot her a look of pure disgust. In the distance I could see Mac's mom, a short woman with dyed blonde hair and heavy makeup applied to her tired-looking face. She was taking baby steps towards her husband and son.

"Ha. This kid is nothing. He's the son of a drunken womanizer—" Mac's dad stared straight into my mom's eyes, "and a lesbian, from what I hear from the kids."

Mac's mom, who was closer to the action now, kind of gasped in disapproval, but neither son nor husband even turned to acknowledge her.

To my mom's credit, she laughed.

I wasn't as forgiving. "She's not a lesbian. Leave her and my dad out of this, okay? Mac and I will solve this problem on the ice."

"What's the problem?" called a voice from behind me.

I turned to see Coach Cal striding towards us. His face was livid with anger as he took in the whole scene. He glanced at the people gathered around us as they edged closer, watching Mac and me and our parents.

"What on earth is going on here?" No one said a word. "Mr. MacDonald? Mrs. Chase?"

"Ms." Spit out Mr. MacDonald, as if it were a swear word.

The coach raised both his hands. "All right. That's enough." He turned to the hockey players, friends, and family who'd gathered to watch the display. "Now, everyone clear out. This is not the example I expect to have set by the parents of the best players on my team."

"My son is the captain of this team," shouted Mr. MacDonald.

"Calm down, Trevor," said Coach Cal.

I glanced at Mac, but then I realized that the coach was talking to Mac's dad. So Mac was Trevor Junior. Oh God. How perfect. Like father, like son.

"I won't calm down. This fairy boy implied that my boy shouldn't be captain. He's the best captain this team has ever had."

The coach shot me a look and I shrugged.

"Chase," Coach Cal said, "get out of here." He turned to my mom. "Ma'am, I would appreciate it if you would take your son home."

My mother nodded. "Zachary wasn't the one causing trouble." She seemed unable to resist adding that little comment.

He gave her a look and she stopped talking.

"Mac and Trevor, you cool off and wait a while before you leave this rink. I won't have parents creating this kind of a fuss again in this arena." He looked around at the kids who'd gathered, shaking his head.

"This is not a good example to be setting for children. You should be ashamed of yourselves. I won't tolerate this behavior from my team. Unfortunately it's the kids who'll have to pay."

We all looked suitably chastised, except for Mac Senior.

Mom tugged on my arm.

I caught sight of Jane moving forward through the crowd, and dug my heels in for a moment. I bent down as if to pick up my bag, but didn't actually grab it.

"Come on, Zachary, let's go." My mom sounded angry.

"Hold on, Mom. Okay?" I said.

Jane reached us. She and Sheila glanced at each other, and then Sheila took a step back. Jane stepped forward to where I stood with my mom.

"He's not worth the trouble, Zachary." She spoke in a soft but clear voice. I stared in her eyes. Once I saw her, I didn't see anyone or anything else.

She took a deep breath. As I stared into the blue of her eyes, I believed I was capable of anything.

"Thanks," she said. She didn't smile, but we both knew what she was talking about.

"Get lost, you little dyke," Mac hissed from behind me.

Before I could reach back and start choking him, Jane lifted her hand and put it on my arm. She shook her head no, her eyes not leaving me, even to glance at Mac. "He's not worth it. Don't even bother with him."

"What the hell did you call my sister?" roared David. He came running towards us from behind Mac's mom.

"Parker, stay out of this." Coach Cal put his hand in the air and shook his head.

"Go," mouthed Jane, still looking right at me. "Thanks, Zachary," Jane said louder so everyone could hear.

I grinned at her, unable for a moment to think of anything to say.

"Zachary, let's go," my mother tugged on my arm.

I glanced around the arena, confused for a moment.

Jane stepped back and sought out her angry brother. Another hockey player held David back from Mac. I glanced around. With a quirky smile, Sheila was helping to hold back David. He seethed, trying to shrug them off.

Mac and his dad watched me like I'd just sprung devil's horns. The other bystanders appeared shocked, thrilled, or both.

Jane glanced at me again as she went towards her brother. She smiled, then she lifted her hand to cover it. Too late. I saw it and smiled back.

I picked up my hockey bag and slung it over my shoulder, then turned and walked out of the arena with my mother tugging my arm.

She didn't say a word until we were both in the car. "What the hell is wrong with you, Zachary?" she spit out as soon as I closed the door behind me. I leaned back in the passenger seat since she'd gripped the keys and jumped in without asking if I wanted to drive. And I knew better than to push it right now.

I didn't say anything for a few seconds and stared out the window. I scanned the parking lot for Jane and David, but didn't see them anywhere.

"He's an asshole, Mom," I said to the window. I smiled, thinking of Jane and the way she'd looked at me.

My mom didn't even yell at me for using that word in front of her. She jammed her key in the ignition. "It's not funny, Zack! And I know he's an asshole." The engine fired up.

I turned from the window, shocked she'd said *asshole*.

She ignored my surprise. "I'm sure that man puts that boy through hell, but the fact is, Mac is the captain." She acted as if she cursed in front of me every day. "You have to try to get along with him. Zack, this is such an important year for you. You can't afford to screw it up. You haven't been putting yourself in the game all season. And now, this. What if there were scouts in the stands today?" She shoulder checked and shifted the car into reverse.

"So what if there were?" I slouched down in my seat, no longer amused by her vanilla cursing. Scouts. Who cared?

She abruptly put her foot on the brake and slammed the car back into park. "What does that mean?" She whirled her head to stare at me.

"I mean that Mac was being an asshole. He gave me a cheap shot, and then his dad practically attacked me in the arena. I need to stand up for myself, instead of checking the stands to see who's watching. It's not the most important thing in the world, you know. I have to look out for myself."

"What are you talking about? Of course it's the most important thing in the world. You want to play hockey, don't you? If scouts were there, they'd have thought you were a hothead. You have to be on guard all the time now." She shook her head, not even able to look at me.

"It was only a practice, Mom. Besides, I am a hothead, in case you haven't noticed."

Her lips pressed tightly together. "You know what I mean."

I turned my attention back to the window. "Maybe it's just not as important to me as it is to you," I said under my breath. And then I held it. I'd never dared voice my doubt about my hockey-playing future to my mom. Not even to myself, for that matter. I kept holding my breath.

She reached over and grabbed my chin, turning my face towards her. I breathed out slowly, shaking her off.

"Zachary. What's going on?" she asked.

"Nothing, Mom. It's just that all you seem to care

about is hockey. Maybe I can do other things, too. Some of those guys are assholes. Is that what you want for me? To become a professional asshole and treat other people like shit?" I wanted to add, just like Dad, but I couldn't do it.

"You know it's what you want. You always have. Anyhow, there're always going to be a few bad apples. I know it's been hard for you, always the new guy, moving around, not having the chance to bond with the boys on your teams, but that's the way professional hockey is, too. You move around a lot and you'll get used to it. The scouts are going to come calling, and you have to be ready for them. You're the only one on your team who is going to make it, you know."

I stared at her and chewed on my lip. Hockey. She took it for granted that it would be my career of choice. Yet she'd used her brains to get by, even though we inherited plenty of money from Dad's untimely death. She hadn't kept contact with anyone from Dad's old hockey life, either. But she kept pushing hockey at me as if it were the most important thing in my life. I couldn't understand why it was so important to her that I play.

"But do I want to, Mom? That's the million-dollar question. Do I want to play hockey the rest of my life? What if I become a big asshole? What if I start disrespecting women or treating them like crap? How much would you like that?"

I wanted to say something to her about those girls in Dad's car when he died. I wanted to tell her about what'd happened with Mona, and ask if she really wanted me to follow in Dad's footsteps in that way, too. But I didn't.

"I don't fit in. And I don't want to fit in." I crossed my arms and stared out at the parking lot. It was nothing exciting to look at, except a bunch of cars and people.

"I don't want to be like him," I said to the window. My teammates were trailing out of the arena now. I thought about myself at the Halloween party. Going after a drunken girl when I had feelings for someone else.

"You didn't know your father, and I'll be sorry about that for every day of your life. But I knew him. He wasn't perfect, but he was a good man. You would have loved him." Mom stayed quiet for a moment. "It's the girl, isn't it?" She finally said. "The one who's always reading books instead of watching the game? There's something going on between you two. I saw it in your face."

I continued staring out the window, shaking my head. How did Mom know my dad wouldn't betray her? Things happened when girls started throwing themselves at you, as I'd just found out. Anyhow, how did she know anything about what I felt for Jane?

"Oh, Zachary. It's her?" She sounded as if I'd done something bad. "That girl is making you question hockey? Just because she doesn't like it?"

I turned to her, furious. "Quit being such a bitch."

We stared at each other. I don't know who was more shocked. Her face turned almost white, and she inhaled deeply and then blew out her breath. I turned to the window. I knew I should apologize, but I couldn't.

We sat in silence for a few minutes.

"Drive out of here, would you please?" I finally snapped. "Everyone's starting to stare at us. Let's just go."

She didn't say anything, but pulled the car out of the parking lot and drove off.

We drove without uttering a word for a few moments.

"I'm sorry," I finally said.

She paused before answering. "She's nothing like Claire," she finally said.

"Thank God. You don't know her, Mom. Jane is brilliant. She's way more than Claire could ever hope to be."

She didn't say anything to that. I wanted to add that she wouldn't sleep with anyone on the hockey team like precious Claire did. But I held back. Some things a guy just can't say to his mom.

She pressed her lips together until they turned white. "Well. I hope she appreciates your hockey. It's the most important thing in your life right now."

"Maybe not." I spoke to the window.

"Don't say that." She sounded as if she was going to cry. "What's going on, Zack? What's the matter with you? Don't worry about what happened today. It was just a blip on the radar. Mac isn't going to keep bugging you. The coach won't allow it to continue. You're far too valuable a player, even when you're not playing full bore, no matter what Mac's father thinks." She shook her head in anger as she thought of Mac Senior.

I wondered what my dad would have done—if he'd have clocked Mr. MacDonald, or if Mr. MacDonald would even have dared to act that way if my dad had been there. I'd kind of hoped Dad would have knocked Mr. MacDonald on his butt if he were still alive.

But the fact was, my dad wasn't around. And I didn't

even mind. I grew up without him and I never knew him. I certainly didn't want to turn out like him, and I didn't know why it was so important to my mom that I did. Look where it got him, dead on the road with a car full of groupies.

My mother didn't realize it, but maybe other things were more important to me than hockey. It really was just a game. And maybe I had other dreams to go after.

CHAPTER

6

A few days later at school, I saw a chance to put my Jane plan into action. I'd been waiting for an opportunity to work at getting closer to Jane, and between classes I spotted her colorful literary friend alone, with Jane nowhere in sight.

"Cassandra?"

I startled the chubby girl by approaching her from behind. With her locker door wide open, I saw posters inside. They almost made a collage. Singers. Pop stars and rock and roll classics. I recognized Sarah McLachlan, a favorite of my mom's. And Jann Arden.

Cassandra turned to look at me, and her eyes scrunched into slits. "Yes?"

"I'm Zack." I hardly sounded brilliant, since I hadn't totally prepared what I would say to break the ice. I smiled. She was prettier up close than I thought. She had a colorful scarf wrapped around her neck; it lit up her face and her green eyes.

"Yeah. I know that. You've been at this school for, like, months already."

"Yeah. I have."

She stared at me. "I totally know all about you from my best friend, too. We both know that, right?" She looked around the hallway, as if she wished someone would rescue her from talking to me.

I'd never taken a chance to approach her before, and of course, she was suspicious. We both knew I wanted to talk about her best friend, Jane. To her, I was just another guy, all caught up in the drama of his own life and oblivious to everyone else.

"I'm not contagious or anything." I said as I leaned against the locker next to hers, grinning.

She just stared at me.

"You look kind of worried," I pointed out. "Like you might catch something from standing near me."

She shook her head and blushed.

"I thought you were awesome in the talent show last week," I said. Blatant flattery, but it also happened to be true. I'd gone to the talent show because my English teacher gave our class extra credit for going, and I'd expected a lame bunch of acts. But this girl's singing talent surprised me. It was extraordinary, and everyone watching knew it. I also thought she was brave, exposing herself to the school like that.

"You should go on *American Idol* or something."

She blushed a deeper red, as if fighting off feeling pleased, just in case I was only teasing her.

I wasn't teasing her but I was on a mission. Since Jane wouldn't talk to me beyond a couple of words, I'd decided on a back door route: get in good with the friend.

"You sounded just like Jann Arden," I said, hoping it was the right thing to say.

"Oh my God," Cassandra said. "You know her? I was totally trying to do her style. You picked that up? You got that?"

Thankfully, I did. I got her style. The girl could wail. The only thing against Cassandra was that she wasn't a size 2. I suspected it would matter. It usually does.

"I play guitar and I sing a little. But nothing like you. You take singing lessons?" I asked.

She shook her head no, but her overly gelled hair didn't move. Her eyes shone with pleasure.

"Sure sounds like you do." I looked right at her, seeing her potential. I wanted to put her on a diet and send her to the gym. Talent only gets you so far. And I was as bad as everyone else, judging her for her weight.

"I'm good at imitating people, but I'm better when I do my own voice," she admitted, then hung her head and reached back into her locker to remove a couple of books.

"Hey, you're good. You know it. Don't be afraid to admit it. That's the way it should be. For example, I know I rock at hockey. Totally. But singing, I'm only average."

She looked at me warily, and then smiled and nodded. "I love performing, despite—" She didn't finish the thought. Then she took a deep breath of air. "I can't believe you really liked it."

"Why not?" I watched as she closed her locker and put the lock back on.

"Well, you know. Like you said. You're a hockey player." She looked around. Time to get to class.

"And . . . ?" I didn't move.

Leaving me standing there would have been rude. I suspected Cassandra wasn't brave enough for rude.

She blushed again. "It's just that, well, most hockey players..." She stopped.

"Didn't go to the concert?" I supplied.

"Not just that. They're such *assholes*." She emphasized the word like she meant it. Like she really, really meant it. Then she caught herself, opening her eyes wide. "Sorry. No offense. I didn't mean. . . I guess, since you sing too..."

I put up my hand. "No. It's okay. You're entitled to your opinion." I grinned and pushed off the locker I'd been leaning on. "There are a lot of assholes out there and some definitely play hockey." I winked. "Anyhow. I just wanted to tell you that I thought you were really good. You have natural talent." I nodded to her locker. "You like Sarah McLachlan?"

She nodded, blushed more. "You know her, too?"

I smiled to indicate I did. I didn't want to say that my mom listened to her. This girl embarrassed pretty easily; she might not think it was cool that she listened to the same music as my parental unit.

"Yeah?" She tilted her head. "Anyhow. You're one to talk. About talent. The way I hear it, every university in the country has an eye on you. Must be nice. Having your life mapped out already."

I grinned. "You know what? It's really not. I don't know what I want to do with my life. I'm fifteen. Hockey is not the only thing I like to do."

She stared at me, understanding in her eyes, but she didn't comment.

"You going to be in the school play?" I asked her as we started walking down the hall. She kept glancing around, as if she shouldn't be seen walking with me.

She shrugged. "In some capacity." She glanced sideways. "Jane, too."

I'd guessed as much. And I was going to be there, too, in some capacity. Because I'd just confirmed that Jane was trying out.

"Me, too. Did I mention that I play the guitar?" I joked.

She smiled quickly and then her face drooped, more serious. "Are you having sex with Mona?" she demanded.

I think I blushed; my face warmed up, anyhow. "No. Uh, I made a stupid mistake at a party. She was drunk, and I was an asshole."

"Hockey player," she pointed out.

I shrugged.

"So you're not?"

I shook my head. "Not."

She shook her head back.

"You're weird, Zack. Just like Jane said."

My eyebrows shot up. "Jane said I was weird?"

"Um. Not so much weird. Different. But I didn't believe her. Maybe now I do. You're not as bad as I thought."

I held back a smile. Mission accomplished! Seemed

like I had her on my side. It wasn't so hard, and she wasn't so bad either.

"Good. Well, okay. I have to get to class," I said. I flashed my teeth in a grin and tilted my head in the other direction. My free period was in the library, at the opposite end of the school.

She clutched her books to her chest. "You like her, don't you?"

I raised an eyebrow.

She examined me. "You do. Take my advice. Don't push her. I think she maybe likes you, but she doesn't trust you yet. Don't you dare tell her I said that, either. She won't even admit it to me. She hates hockey players, you know. And she's very reserved around guys—all guys." She looked conspiringly around the hallway at the kids whizzing past, none of them giving us the time of day. Leaning closer to me, she said: "She has her reasons." I could smell Bubble Yum on her breath.

"What reasons?"

She straightened, looking around again. "I gotta get to class. See ya!" She started hurrying off, then glanced back over her shoulder.

"Hurt her, and I'll chop off your jock strap—" she grinned, "while it's still on." She giggled and took off.

I watched her go. It seemed like she was on my side, but she hadn't given me the secret handshake. It didn't necessarily make things any easier with Jane.

"Whazzup, Chase? Goin' after the fat chicks now?" I recognized Mac's voice behind me. Male laughter accompanied his comment.

I turned. As usual, Eddie and Cole were standing there with Mac. They all watched, amused by their ring-leader. Mac's eyes brimmed with hostility. I checked to see if Cassandra heard his insult, but luckily she'd disappeared into the crowded hallway. I hoped like hell she hadn't picked up on his ignorant comment. She didn't deserve Mac's wrath just because of me.

I didn't bother answering Mac. Defending Cassandra to him was useless, and it would only call more attention to her—attention I knew she wouldn't want.

I nodded to the guys and started walking away from them towards my class.

"You poking that meaty thing with your sausage? I'd think even you could do better than Cassandra, dude. And Mona's got the hots for you. She's already done most of the hockey team, but at least you could get some from a girl who's got nice tits and a firm ass. Not a giant pork rind like that one." Mac's loud voice drew attention in the still congested hallway.

The other guys laughed. I stopped walking and turned around, lifting my middle finger and giving Mac the well-known salute.

"Ouch," Mac grabbed at his heart, following behind me. "The pretty boy likes fat girls and dykes. You gonna defend her honor, too, or do you only do that when your mommy is around to protect you?"

I could feel the shift in the crowd. I heard audible in-takes of breath, gasps. There was a buzzing excitement in the air. Without even thinking, I dropped my books and charged him.

I connected with Mac's chin as he punched me in the stomach. The air sucked right out of me, and for a moment, I stumbled. Then I righted myself and went after him with a roar.

In the background I heard yelling and chaos, along with shouts of "Zack Attack!" But the only thing I focused on was Mac. I wanted to punch him and hurt him. Man, he was evil. Pure evil.

Someone grabbed both my arms and held them behind me, not even struggling to do so. I growled in anger.

"Cut it out this instant!" a voice hissed in my ear. Louder, he said, "Zachary Chase, what the hell is going on here?"

It was my English teacher, Mr. Wright, who also happened to be the Vice Principal. Just my luck. And, even though he stood a couple inches shorter than me, he looked like he was chiseled out of pure muscle, a real wrestler. He held me with very little effort.

Facing me, Mac wiped blood off his mouth with the back of his hand. Good. At least I'd made him bleed.

"Get out of here, all of you! Get to class, *now*." As if on cue, the bell rang to signify new classes were beginning. The kids in the hallway scrambled, hurrying to get to class; they were still buzzing with the excitement of our fight.

Mr. Wright still held my arms behind me; I stopped struggling, but kept my focus on Mac.

"He's crazy," Mac said. "He came after me for no reason. This guy's seriously unstable." Beside him, Cole and Eddie nodded in agreement.

"Zip it, Trevor. God knows you've never provoked anyone in your life." Mr. Wright's voice was filled with sarcasm. Thank God.

"You two. Beat it," he said to Mac's tag-a-longs. They sped down the hall without looking back.

Mr. Wright let me go. I restrained myself from charging Mac again. I was mad, but not completely stupid. Mr. Wright jerked his head.

"Office," he growled.

We had little choice but to follow.

"Asshole," I muttered to Mac under my breath.

Mr. Wright whipped his head around. I smiled and said nothing more.

When we reached the office, he held the door open and we stepped inside. The secretary sat behind her desk, tapping at computer keys. She peered up at us, over the top of her reading glasses. Then she glanced at Mr. Wright.

"You need to use the principal's office? Mr. Kirby's still at the school board."

He nodded. She took her fingers off the computer, pulled open her desk drawer, and took out a key. She picked it up, holding it with high regard, and rose from her chair. We followed behind her. I looked at the wrinkles in her dress. She was gray haired and old, and getting frail. A peach sweater was tied around her shoulders.

She opened the principal's office door and let us all in.

Mr. Wright bellowed, "Get in and sit down. Both of you. You're lucky Mr. Kirby isn't around today." He walked behind Mr. Kirby's desk and glared at both of us as we sat in the seats in front of the desk. "You two are on the same hockey team, aren't you?"

We didn't look at each other, but nodded.

"So what the hell is going on?" He sat in Mr. Kirby's chair.

Neither of us spoke.

"Trevor?"

"I have no idea, Mr. Wright. I was in the hallway, minding my own business and Zack charged me for no reason."

"Mr. Chase?"

"There's a little more to it than that." I flexed my hands into fists.

"Well?"

I didn't answer. I wasn't going to say anything about Cassandra, Jane, or my mom.

"Did you charge him in the hallway?" Mr. Wright asked.

I nodded. I mean, I had. Why deny the truth?

He raised his hand as if to flick away a bug. "Mr. MacDonald. Get your ass out of here. Do not gloat. Do not think you are getting away with anything. I have noted this, and I am watching you. Another incident and your father will be called in. Understand? And I know how much you don't want that."

Mac nodded and shot up out of the chair.

Mr. Wright waved again towards the door, and Mac disappeared in record time, slamming the door behind him.

The silence in the room was overwhelming.

"You want to fill me in?" Mr. Wright finally asked, when I thought I would choke if he didn't say something.

I shook my head, but looked him in the eye.

"You don't tell me what's going on, I have no choice but to call your mother." He leaned back in the chair, watching me.

I nodded. He didn't say anything for a few seconds, then he leaned forward.

"Kids giving you a rough time? Being the new guy?" His voice softened. He was talking to me now as a person.

"I've been at this school for a few months already. I'm not the new guy anymore." I didn't want his pity.

He continued to stare at me.

"You're not going to tell me what happened?"

I didn't answer.

"Mac's got a lot of pressure on him. His dad is a hockey fanatic. Mac's been the king for a long time," he said.

I blinked, surprised.

"Don't look so shocked. I hear kids talking." He stood up and moved to the front of the desk, sitting on the edge of it. "I hear you're an awesome hockey player."

I shrugged again.

"Heard you're going all the way. Your natural talent might threaten some guys, eh? Parents too?"

I wondered what he'd heard. Obviously quite a lot. I shrugged again. He watched me without comment for a while. I kept my face neutral. He leaned back.

"Tell you what, Zachary. I was going to call your mom, but I'm going to give you a break. For being the new guy. Takes a lot longer than a few months not to be the new guy in a town this size." He paused, and then flicked his hand towards the door. "Okay, Mr. Chase, get the hell out of this office."

I looked at him, dumbstruck.

"Get out, Zachary. Now. Before I change my mind. And keep your nose out of trouble from now on. Try to get along with Mac. He's been the leader of the hockey world his whole life. You're really freaking him out."

I stood.

He winked. "I was a fan—of your dad. It was terrible, what happened to him."

I nodded, looked away. "Uh. Thanks, Mr. Wright."

"Things aren't always what they appear to be, you know."

I shrugged.

"All right. See you in English."

I turned to go, my hand on the doorknob when he spoke again.

"You enjoying it?" he called.

I looked back at him. Puzzled. I just wanted to get out.

"English."

"Um. Yeah. It's my favorite subject actually."

He nodded. "You've got an aptitude for it, you know. You're a really good writer."

"My mom's good at it, too."

He nodded again. God, did everyone in this town know everything about each other?

Apparently. I twisted the knob. "It's a good skill to have. Keep your options open. You know, in case hockey doesn't work out."

I nodded, thinking of something else. "You run the school musical, right?" I asked.

He nodded, a small smile on his face. "Every year. Why? You trying out?"

I shrugged. "I play guitar."

He laughed out loud. “Sorry, Zack. No offense. It’s just that I don’t think I’ve ever seen a hockey player in this town try out. You’re not like most of the kids in Haletown.” He leaned back on the desk, a smile on his face. It made him look younger. Like someone I might want to hang with.

“So I keep hearing.”

His smile widened. “It’s not an insult, you know. Be who you are. Don’t let other people dictate your choices for you.”

I nodded as he stood, pondering his words. Who did I listen to? What did I want? Did I even know?

“You need a note to get into class?” he asked.

“I have a study period.” I hesitated. “Um. Thanks.”

“Get out of here.”

He didn’t have to tell me a third time. I hurried out of the office, taking a deep breath in the hallway. That was a near miss.

“What the hell are you up to?” hissed someone behind me.

I recognized Jane’s voice and spun on my heels. She stood in the hallway, her arms crossed, watching me. In camouflage pants and black T-shirt, she looked like a small rebel. She clutched a handful of books to her chest, her backpack straps visible on her shoulders.

I looked around. The hallway was otherwise empty.

“Um, what do you mean?”

“I heard you were asking Cassandra questions about me.”

“Shouldn’t you be in class?” I asked.

She didn't answer. "I also heard you and Mac were going at it in the hallway. That have anything to do with me?" She didn't wait for an answer. "Stay out of it, okay? You don't have to keep rescuing me. I've been living in this place a long time."

I nodded. "I know. Anyhow, my fight with Mac wasn't about you."

She stared at me. "You sure?" She didn't drop her eyes. "I heard he's been telling everyone about Halloween." Her eyes narrowed. "About me, not you. Except his version of what happened is a little different from the truth."

My hands clenched into fists. "I'll kill him."

"I don't think so. Why do you care anyway, Zachary? What's it matter to you?" She titled her head, clearly puzzled.

"I don't like guys who take advantage of girls." My voice sounded stiff, stupid.

"Then you shouldn't do it either."

I nodded. "You're right. If you mean Mona, it was a mistake."

She didn't say anything, watched me without blinking. "You should leave her alone. She's not what you think she is."

"I'm not interested in Mona." I stared back.

Her face colored and she looked away. "Yeah, well. You should leave Mac alone, too, and for good reason."

"He doesn't scare me."

"Apparently. Anyhow, it's not your problem where I'm concerned. I can take care of myself, you know."

I grinned. "I know."

"Yeah? So what's with the damsel in distress thing? I'm a big girl." She shifted her feet and seemed to be studying mine.

I stared at her until she looked up. Then I took a deep breath. It was now or never. The back door hadn't worked too well. I needed to knock at the front.

"I like you," I said.

Her face crumpled as if she'd swallowed a bitter drink. She lowered her glance to the floor. Quickly she looked up again, her eyes flashing. "No you don't. You like Mona."

"No. You."

"Why?"

"God. Why wouldn't I?" I brushed back my hair.

"Well, for starters, look at you, and look at me."

I didn't say anything, but raised an eyebrow to signify, "So what?"

"You don't even know me. You're a jock. I'm not. You play hockey. You made out with Mona. I heard you and she—" She stopped.

"Not true," I told her.

"What? That you don't play hockey?"

I smiled. "There's nothing going on with me and Mona."

"That's not what it looked like to me."

"It was nothing. I have my eye on someone else."

"Nice way of showing it."

"You're right. I apologize. But I'm not interested in her. Just you." I wondered if she was a little bit jealous. I hoped so.

She shifted back and forth and looked around again. I could tell she was about to bolt.

"Tell you what. Since you think I don't even know you, how about giving me a chance to find out?"

She shook her head. "No."

"I dare you. I think you're afraid."

I saw a gleam in her eye. Good. Just as competitive as her brother.

"One coffee. Let me show you what a great guy I am. And I'll promise not to rescue you ever again."

"You don't drink coffee. You're a jock."

I grinned. "For you, I might."

She shook her head.

"I dared you," I reminded her.

"You think that matters?"

"I do. I'll tell everyone you're too chicken to take a dare from a hockey player. I'll tell everyone you're secretly in love with me."

She bit her lower lip. "I am not secretly in love with anybody."

"I swear I'll do it. I'll spread the rumor all over school," I grinned.

"I can't believe I'm going to let you push me into this."

I smiled, happy with her response. "I won't bite, I promise. Just coffee. No, make that hot chocolate."

"Just like David." She shook her head. "Of course he prefers his hot chocolate with a couple ounces of Malibu Rum these days." Her voice sounded angry. "You know what? I will have a hot chocolate with you. I accept your dare. I am not afraid of any hockey player."

I swallowed my happiness, coolly waiting until she began walking towards the school exit. Then I fell in step beside her. We strolled together down the hallway and headed out the front doors.

"You worried about David?" I asked when we stepped outside into the unseasonably warm autumn air.

"Perceptive jock, aren't you?" She smiled slightly, taking the edge off her words. "Yeah. I do worry about him. His drinking, I mean. It's gotten worse since he lost his license. He's out of control and my parents don't even see it. They think the best way to handle it is to make me his personal chaperone. As if I can stop him. He's crazy, and it's worse since he's gotten involved with Candy. She's no good for him."

I listened without comment.

She stopped walking for a moment. "You know, Zack, Mac is not a good person to have as an enemy," she blurted out.

She shrugged off her backpack, unzipped it, and stuffed her books inside. I held out my hand to take it from her, but she shook her head and put the backpack back on. "Forget it. I can carry it myself." She started walking again.

"That the voice of experience?" I asked. "Is Mac an enemy of yours?"

"I can handle Mac," she told me.

"I don't think you should have to."

"I can handle him." She walked fast, and I adjusted my stride to keep with her.

"Like I said, I don't think you should have to. I'm not

going to stand by and let him do anything to intimidate you or anyone else."

She glanced up at me, and there was something in her face I couldn't read.

I touched her arm and stopped walking. "I'm too late, aren't I?" I asked.

She stopped, then started moving again, but avoided looking at me. "Mac's a pig. But don't try to fight my battles. I'll handle him myself. His dad, though, he's a psycho. He doesn't like you. He can make things really hard for you."

I laughed. "His dad? I don't think so. I don't want to brag, but I do okay on the ice, you know."

"I know you're good, Zachary. But Mac's dad is crazy."

"Oh? How do you know I'm good?" I teased. "You never actually watch me play. You're always reading those books of yours in the stands."

She ducked her head. "There was a time that I really liked hockey." Her eyes widened a little, as if she couldn't believe she'd just said the words out loud. "I should. I've grown up in a friggin' hockey rink watching David. I even used to play. But now I hate it. I hate it."

I decided not to push. This girl didn't invite interference.

"Is that right? Well, I'm kind of indifferent these days."

She looked up, rolling her eyes. "You? You probably poop hockey pucks."

I laughed. "Uh, no. Actually I don't. But, you want to know a secret?"

She nodded.

I grinned. "I might go after the captain position."

Her eyes widened. "You can't! Mac's always been captain."

I shrugged. "Things change. Seems to me, everyone in this town lets him get away with things. Too many things. Maybe Coach Cal wants to shake things up."

We stopped on the curb to cross the street leading to the coffee shop in the strip mall.

"You're either really brave or really stupid," Jane said.

"What do you think?"

She glanced up at me. "It's a toss-up. I hope you're not stupid."

I nodded. Smiled. "Nope, I'm not stupid. That's a start, right?"

I opened the door to the coffee shop, holding it for her. She stared at me before walking in. "Where did you get your manners? You for real, Zachary?"

I laughed. "Why does everyone keep asking me that question?"

"I guess you're not like most other guys, that's all."

"Isn't that a good thing?" I asked as she slipped by me. I smelled vanilla in her hair.

She shrugged.

I followed her into the coffee shop to a line. Despite her protests, I paid for her hot chocolate and we grabbed a table for two and sparred. I didn't even feel nervous finally able to talk to her. She kept me on my toes, and she even made me laugh.

When we got on the topic of Mr. Wright, Jane told

me she thought he was great. I sipped at my hot chocolate, waiting for the right time to jump in and tell her I might try out for the school play.

Even with my back to the door, I heard the unmistakable squeal of girls coming into the place. Jane's eyes darkened.

"Jane and Zack Attack. Isn't this interesting," a high-pitched voice called out from across the room.

I turned as Candy rushed towards us, dressed in a tight pair of jeans and a tiny T-shirt. Behind her were a couple of girls. I watched them all approach. Mona wore a short plaid skirt and tiny tank top. Her eyes scanned the coffee shop, trying not to land on us. I couldn't tell if she was embarrassed or pissed off.

"Last thing I heard, you were pounding on Mac in the hallway, and now you're cozying up with Janie?" Candy glanced back at her groupies. "Is this totally creepy, or what? What do you think, Mona? Is your boy making his moves on my sister-in-law? Now, I heard you were, like, a little odd, Zack, but Jane? This is just way over the top. What do you think, Mona?"

Mona didn't answer. She hung back as if she wanted to be anywhere else in the world. I wondered what was wrong with her. People said she had a crush on me, so maybe she was uncomfortable seeing me with Jane. Something wasn't right about her expression, though. She didn't look jealous; she looked like she wanted to disappear. This didn't look like the same girl who'd promised me a blow job a couple weeks ago. I wondered if she was on something.

Candy grabbed Mona's skinny bare arm and pulled her towards our table. Mona looked into my eyes and then quickly at Jane.

"Candy," Jane said, "since you're so catty, why don't you order a bowl of milk from the front counter, okay? Zachary and I are friends. We're having coffee. Just take a chill pill, okay?" She avoided looking at Mona.

Candy crossed her arms and glared at her. "Be nice or I might have to tell David you're being mean to me again."

Candy allowed Mona to drag her to the front counter.

Jane shook her head. "I can't believe my brother has the hots for that girl. She's totally evil."

I watched her. "Chill pill?"

She smiled, shrugged.

"So. Are we really friends, Jane? Cause you gotta know . . . I meant what I said—" I let my words hang in the air, unfinished.

Her face changed. She turned red and didn't look me in the eye.

That's what I thought. I didn't say it out loud.

"Did you hook up with Mona after the Halloween party or not?" she asked, still not meeting my gaze.

I shrugged.

She glanced up. "I heard you did."

"Didn't." I smiled.

She caught it, and a grin tugged at the corners of her mouth. "Because I wouldn't want you to catch anything." She frowned then, and glanced back to the front counter. "They're total lushes. Drinking all the time. Candy is a major bad influence on David."

"Mona was the one so drunk at Mac's Halloween party." I looked over at Mona and Candy.

"I know. I saw her. She's been on a downward spiral ever since seventh grade." Jane followed my glance to Mona. Mona looked almost gloomy.

"Oh?"

Jane turned back to me. "We used to be really good friends. When we were younger."

"Really?" I looked back at Mona and then at Jane, with my eyebrows raised.

"She was different back then. So was I. People change." Her facial expression hardened a little. The subject officially closed. She checked her watch.

"I should get back to school. I have a class . . . . "

I tried not to show my disappointment. I'd been making progress, but for some reason, she'd closed off again. Shut me out.

Seemed like there was history I wasn't supposed to know. Jane stood up and I joined her. We walked to the trashcan and dumped our paper cups. I moved to the front door and held it open.

She rolled her eyes. "I'm pretty strong. I can even open doors myself sometimes. You always hold doors open for girls?"

I shrugged. "My mom freaks if I don't."

She slipped past me. She smelled like a girl, softer than she appeared with her dark hair and clothes. We strolled back to the school in a slower, compatible silence.

Before we reached the front doors I blocked her. Looking down at her, I took a quick breath. "You want to go out with me sometime?"

She hid a smile, her cheeks pinkened. Good signs, as far as I knew. I honestly didn't know what her answer would be.

"Maybe," she said. She turned and ran to the front doors, zipped up the steps, and disappeared inside, just as a group of girls burst through the doors. They spread out in front of me and I couldn't see Jane any longer.

"What are you smiling about, Zack?"

Sheila. She stood in front of me on the top step, her long auburn curls piled on top of her head, her hands on her hips. Her eyebrows were scrunched up and her face appeared shadowy.

"Zachary Chase, from what I just heard, you were in a fight with Mac in the hallway. That's nothing to smile about."

"Hey, Sheila, I already have a mother," I called up.

"Oh, I'll give you more shit than your mother." She glared at me. "Did I just see Jane fly by me? That have anything to do with your goofy smile?"

"Bug off, Sheila." The other girls giggled, enjoying the show.

Sheila stepped down the stairs and stood beside me, her neck stretching back to look me in the eye. "Zack. What on earth were you doing with Mac? Are you trying to commit social suicide?"

"Social suicide?" I started up the stairs and she followed close on my heels.

"Mac runs things around here. You may not like it, but you have to accept it—at the rink and at school. He hates your guts. He'll make things pretty hard for you."

"I think it's too late for that. You want me to be afraid of him?"

She made a face.

"You think he's a better hockey player than I am?"

She shook her head vigorously, rushing behind me to keep up with her short legs. "That's not the point."

"No. The point is this. He's a bully. Maybe worse. He has no respect for anyone but himself. I don't like the way he leads the hockey team, and I really don't like the way he treats the girls in this town." I made a sharp turn around a corner towards my next class. Sheila stayed on me.

"It's not your job to stop it. It's been going on a long time."

"Well, someone has to try. It might as well be me. What do I have to lose?" I stopped and Sheila crashed right into me.

"Yeah. Think about what you have to lose." Sheila said, then sighed dramatically.

I stepped away from her. I wasn't afraid of Mac, and I wasn't going to conform or pretend to go along with him just to make things easy for myself. After all, who ever said things were going to be easy?

David Parker sprinted up behind us in the hallway and slapped my back. I stopped but Sheila kept moving, practically running down the hallway to get away from us. Funny the way my tough friend acted around him. Like she was nervous.

"Hey, man. How's it going?" David asked, as he leaned against the locker behind him. He watched me closely.

In spite of myself, I tensed up, as if I was about to be quizzed about my future aspirations or my intentions towards his sister.

"Good. What's up, dude?" I raised my brows and tried to look relaxed, instead of like I'd just asked out his twin sister.

He didn't say anything for a minute. I shifted my feet a little and ran my fingers through my hair.

"Uh. I wanted to ask a favor of you, actually," he said.

I breathed out. "Oh?"

He looked around the hallway to see if anyone was listening. The crowd was dwindling down as kids scrambled to class. "You're an okay guy. And I need some help from someone who doesn't have a big mouth. You know what I mean?"

I didn't answer him yet. The buzzer rang and I glanced around the now empty hall. I was late for class. I didn't even have my books out of my locker yet. On the spot, I decided to ditch it. A skip on my record was worth a date with David Parker's sister. Well, kind of a date.

"The thing is . . . well, my parents are kind of freaking on me. About my drinking, I mean, you know? I do like to party a little too much. And I'm trying to get it under control." He looked down the floor and then glanced around at everything in the hallway—except at me.

"So. I thought, you could, you know, maybe make sure I don't get too plastered at parties with the boys? You know?" He kept his voice low and avoided looking at me, embarrassed.

I stared at him. "What?"

He pushed off the lockers. "You know. Just make sure I don't drink too much. If I look really drunk, don't let anyone feed me any more liquor."

"Um. David. You could probably just try drinking less."

He laughed, but his face stiffened up. "No. I mean it, man. Once I get going, it's like I have no control anymore. I just keep on drinking until I'm out of it. I thought, since you're usually the most sober guy around, you could keep an eye out for me—without making a big deal about it."

"Maybe you should try just having one drink. Or maybe only two."

He looked at me like I was the crazy one. "Would you mind just doing it, man? My parents are going to freak if I come home totally out of it one more time. I'm on a short leash. It's just for the next couple of parties."

I shrugged. "I'll do what I can, bro."

He nodded. "Cool. Thanks, man. And I'd appreciate it if you kept this, you know, under your hat."

I lifted my fingers and pretended to zip my lips. He clunked my knuckles and turned to walk in the opposite direction.

"See ya, Zack Attack."

I watched him leave.

The guy clearly owned a drinking problem. I didn't know what I could do to help. I wanted to, but I also wanted to be on the good side of his sister. How I handled this would depend a lot on Jane.

7

In hockey, sometimes a good pass, or a set of passes, can be as much fun as scoring. It's like magic when you skate right through traffic, bouncing the puck off a teammate—even Mac. *Wham*! He got a clean poke into an empty net as the goalie dove the crease on a fake. A play that would stick with me.

Next shift.

"Oof."

I fell to the ice, automatically curling up into a fetal position. I couldn't breathe. In the background I heard a whistle blow, and then the referee was down on his knee, right in my face.

"You okay, kid?" he said.

I couldn't answer him because I couldn't catch my breath.

Mac's face appeared over me. He bent down on one knee. His dark eyes were little slits in his face. I wondered if I was hallucinating. He looked exactly like the devil. He leaned in closer.

"This is just a little taste of things to come. Get on my

bad side and the team won't be looking out for you. Accidents are bound to happen," Mac said.

He stood up, and in the distance, I heard him arguing with the ref, shouting about penalty shots and the unfairness of the hit I'd taken. Bastard.

I lay still. The world whirled around me and I tried to catch my breath and get my wind back.

Coach Cal bent near my face. "Chase? You okay?" He disappeared and I heard him shouting. "Get the paramedics out here. He's out of it."

"No," I managed to whisper. "I'm okay."

The coach got down on both knees. "Can you get up?"

I shook my head.

"Mac. Get over here. Help him up."

I moaned my displeasure, but Coach didn't hear it, or else didn't understand my reaction. It was Mac's job as captain to help me.

Mac leaned down again. "You stupid prick. This is only the beginning," he whispered right into my face.

"Parker, help me get him up," he shouted behind him.

Mac slid an arm under one of my armpits. David came and lifted me on the other side. With my head down, gritting my teeth in pain, the two of them helped me skate off the ice and into the box. I heard light applause from the crowd.

"Take him to the locker room!" Coach Cal ordered the boys.

I shook my head. "No. I'll be okay."

Mac spoke into my ear. "I know a goon on every team in this league, Chase. You're going down."

I fumbled my way onto the bench and sat still, trying to catch my breath.

"Maybe I will go to the locker room," I said to the assistant coach a few minutes later.

Coach Cal leapt back up on the bench and watched the players as the action resumed.

"You need some help?" the assistant asked.

I nodded and the two of us walked slowly down the hallway to the locker room. Inside, I lay on my back and caught my breath.

I'd never been in pain like this before. I wanted to cry. I didn't even see who had sucker-punched me, but he'd hit me harder than I'd ever been hit before. I'd been standing alone, prowling the blue zone, but the play was in someone else's hands. From nowhere I'd been charged, and a stick had been buried deep into my ribs.

I sat up and tried to peel off my equipment. I touched my ribs tenderly and sucked in my breath. There had to be something broken in there.

It took me a good half hour to get my clothes on.

By the time I finished changing, the guys came whooping into the locker room. They were howling and making a lot of noise.

"Nice pass, Mac," Cole said, as he dropped onto the bench. "Hey, Zack Attack, you pussy. Couldn't even get your ass back out to watch us win our first game in two weeks? I scored the winning goal. Smoked it right in off a pass from Mac."

"Pussy is right," Mac said. "Need some tissues for your tears?"

"Knock it off!" Coach Cal shouted at Mac as he came into the locker room. "Chase. How you feelin'?"

Suck it up. That was the rule. "Fine. I'm fine, Coach."

I didn't get up or move. I sat in place, slumped against the wall, with half a grimace, half a smile as the guys bragged about their moves on the ice and made fun of the other team. Soon enough, as always, the talk turned to girls.

"Zack, you see Mona and Candy in the stands?" David said. "Come out with us. Mona is hot and she wants you, man. She wants you bad. She'll kiss your belly better. And a whole lot more."

I didn't have the strength to comment. I thought he probably wanted me to baby-sit his drinking and I really wasn't up for it.

"Whatsamatter, Parker? You haven't heard the news?"

David glanced at Mac, who'd jumped into the conversation uninvited. I saw a sinister smile on Mac's face.

"He wants to do your sister," Mac said.

David's face turned ashen and he looked over at me. His face swam in front of my eyes. "What is he talking about, Zack?"

"It's nothing," I managed to squeak out. "Jane and I are friends. I might take her out."

Mac stood up. He put both arms in front of him and made the motion of humping with his hips, his face a contortion and his arms flailing back and forth, simulating sex.

I ignored him and the howls of the guys. "Don't worry about it, we're cool," I said to David. My voice was barely above a whisper.

David stared at me. "She hates hockey players."

"I know," I said.

"That's why she digs Chase," Mac said, mocking my strained voice and laughing. "She knows he's a big suck ass on the ice. Guy can't even see a body check coming. Your sister loves him for his sensitive side."

"That was not a body check," I said through clenched teeth. The pain was grating on my nerves. I wished Mac would shut up or go away.

"I can't believe you want to take out my sister," said David, beside me.

I made an exerted effort and grinned. "She's nothing like you, that's why I like her." I waited a minute to monitor his reaction. At least he wasn't freaking out. "You cool with it?"

Mac made choking noises. "He's asking for permission to screw Parker's sister," he shouted to the other players.

He didn't even see David charge him. The locker room went crazy. Bodies flew and shoved. Bones crunched. Eddie yanked David off Mac, but he flew at him again. The noise increased as guys shouted at them and each other. Then Coach Cal's booming voice shut everyone up.

"Mac!" he hollered. "Get out of here. *Now*. Take your equipment and go—no lip."

Mac frothed, but he left the locker room quietly and willingly. Before he pushed the door open to leave, he turned to David and winked at him. He looked at me and lifted his middle finger.

Coach Cal walked over to where I sat. “What’s going on with you two?”

“Hey, he’s not the one who just charged Mac, Coach. That was me,” David said, sticking up for me.

“I know, David. I made a note of it. Trouble is, I don’t think any of this would be going on if it weren’t for Zachary.”

I didn’t say anything.

“What do you have to say for yourself?” Coach Cal sounded pissed.

I tried to stand up. I didn’t say anything. Because I passed out.

When I woke up, my mom was smoothing the hair back off my face. I opened my eyes and she smiled at me.

“Zachary,” she said. “Hey, you scared me, kid.”

I felt a little scared myself, with no idea where I was or how much time had passed.

“Where am I?” I tried turning my head, but it hurt to move it.

“In an ambulance. We’re on our way to the hospital. They think your ribs are broken.”

I closed my eyes. It still hurt like hell. Something was definitely wrong.

“Zachary?”

My mom’s voice sounded different. Scared.

“I’m okay. It just hurts.” I didn’t open my eyes. I lay still, feeling the motion of the ambulance as we drove.

I wondered if the lights were flashing as we sped down the highway.

She grabbed my hand and squeezed it.

"Hockey's not going so good this year," I said to her, my eyes still closed.

"You're going to be okay, Zachary. It'll mean taking a month or so off to heal, but you've got a little bit of time. You'll be back in time for the playoffs."

I didn't answer her. It wasn't what I meant. I wanted to tell her I didn't want to play in the playoffs. I didn't want to be on a team where Mac was captain. He was a bad kid. It was bad karma. It wasn't important to me to be the best player on this team. I didn't want to fight someone like Mac. There were other things that mattered to me more. Like Jane, like my own life.

I thought about the school musical and hoped I still could try out for it. It was weird. It never interested me before, and at first I'd considered it just to get closer to Jane, but I realized I actually wanted to be in it—for me.

"Maybe I'll be in the school musical while I heal." I smiled.

I didn't open my eyes, but I could feel my mom's surprise.

"The musical?"

"The school's putting on *Grease*."

She didn't say anything. I opened my eyes. "Mom?"

She touched my hand. "No. It's okay, Zachary. I don't think you're going to be able to move around enough to star in a show." She paused. "You know your dad was in *his* school play."

"He was?" That threw me.

"I never saw it, obviously. It was before we met. But he told me about it. He was really proud, even though the guys tormented him. He told me about it after we'd been dating for a while. I was teasing him about being an uncultured hockey player, and he told me he was a thespian under his hockey equipment."

I nodded, closed my eyes again. I'd never known that about my dad. More of his blood. I frowned. I'd thought this interest came from me. I'd have to rethink trying out for the show.

The ambulance bumped and I inhaled sharply, as a pain shot through my insides.

"We're almost at the hospital," said a female voice. I looked up. A paramedic was seated behind my mom. I hadn't even noticed her.

"Thank God," I said.

Mom grasped my hand tighter. "You're so much like him, you know."

"I'm nothing like him."

Her voice sounded far away. "No, you are. You have his strengths, you know. Everything good about him." She sighed. "I loved him so much. You're becoming the man your father was."

I couldn't think of anything to say. I mean, what do you say to that? I didn't want to live out his life for her. I didn't want to be anything like him. I wouldn't ever do to my wife what he did to her.

A few minutes later, they wheeled me out of the ambulance and into a hallway while my mom filled out papers to admit me. I lay on a gurney for a while, waiting for X-rays that eventually revealed cracked ribs. Since they weren't broken, it allayed our fear that they could puncture my lungs. I would be fine. Sore, but fine.

I would be out of commission for at least four weeks, the doctor said. No skating. Nothing athletic until that time had passed. They taped me up and sent me hobbling slowly out the door.

When we walked out of the examination room and back into the emergency area to leave, I stopped.

Jane was curled up in a chair, reading a book. She was engrossed in it. I glanced at my mom. She shrugged.

"Jane," I called out.

Jane jumped up. When she spotted me, a smile lit up her face. Even in her Goth makeup and dark clothes, she was the most beautiful girl I'd ever seen. A rebellious one, but the real deal.

She unfolded her legs and stood, sneaking a shy look at my mother as she walked towards us.

"Hello, Mrs. Chase," she said.

"Hello, Jane. You drove all this way by yourself?" my mom asked.

Jane just nodded.

My mom glanced down at her watch. "I'll go and grab a coffee from the snack bar, okay, Zachary? I'll be back in five minutes."

That's another reason I like my mom. She knows when to take a hike. I nodded. Jane and I stood quietly for a moment, watching Mom leave.

"Your mom is beautiful," Jane said.

I turned my attention to Jane. "So are you."

She blushed and seemed to find her feet fascinating. "I am not. She looked back into my eyes. "Anyway, how are you? Are you okay?" We stood in place. Moving would have hurt too much. Around us, people were sitting on uncomfortable blue chairs, waiting to see the doctors.

"Cracked ribs. I'll live. It feels like I got stabbed, but I'm going to make it. I can't believe you drove all this way to see me."

She ignored that. "It was a dirty hit," she said instead. Her lips were pinched into a thin line, her brows creased.

I tilted my head and shrugged. It was, but what could I say? I was more interested that she'd made the drive to the hospital to see me.

"Mac's behind it." Jane's voice was hard, bitter.

I knew that was true, but wondered why she was so certain. "Why do you say that?"

"That's the way he operates. He's dirty. He gets other people to do his bad deeds for him." She shook her head, definitely angry.

I shrugged. "No one can prove anything."

"No. And that's exactly the way Mac likes things. I knew he was going to do something like this."

She chewed on her lip and I watched, feeling a little envious.

"You came to see me," I said again, to change the subject. I didn't want to talk about Mac anymore.

She smiled. It was the kind of smile that turns guys' insides to mush.

"I kind of feel like it's my fault. So I wanted to make sure you're okay."

"You drove by yourself?"

She nodded again. "David went home with Candy. I told him to tell Mom and Dad that I was coming here to see how you were."

"David was okay with that?" I asked. I wasn't sure how David would react to news of Jane visiting me, especially after what Mac had told him.

She flashed her smile again. I felt like a girl, with the way my insides reacted—all nervous and twitchy. Must have been something to do with the pain medication the doctor gave me.

"David was fine with it."

"Mac told him I was interested in you." I watched for her reaction.

"Are you?" She melted my heart the way she looked at me.

"Very."

"I hate hockey players, you know," she said softly, with the slightest hint of a smile.

I ignored a pang in my gut. "I guess I'm pretty much *not* playing hockey for a while."

"I know." She licked her lips.

"So will you go out with me?"

"Maybe." Her expression was almost demure.

"A pity date?" I asked her.

We both grinned. I was about to risk further injury and lean forward to kiss her when my mom's voice broke into our private little world.

"Um, Zachary. You ready to go?"

I didn't turn to look at her, I could tell by her voice she

was right behind me. It would have caused too much pain under the circumstances, or else I would have given her a dirty look.

"Jane's got a car," I said, raising my eyebrows hopefully at Jane.

Her eyes opened wide and she shook her head.

"Not this time. I want to get you home." Mom stepped into our circle so she stood beside me. "Thanks for coming, Jane. To make sure Zachary's okay. But I'd like to take him home myself. Make sure there're no complications."

Jane bobbed her head up and down. "Of course, Mrs. Chase. I didn't expect to drive him home after what's happened. I just wanted to come, you know, to make sure he was okay."

My mom forced a smile. "We appreciate it. Well. Let's go, shall we, Zack? You want me to get you a wheelchair?"

"I can walk, Mom. Where are you parked, Jane?"

She pointed to the parking lot in front of the building.

"I'll go get the car. Your aunt dropped it off, and I'll bring it to the front entrance. Can you walk him to the entrance, Jane, and make sure he's okay?" my mom asked.

When Jane agreed, Mom hurried off.

I began my slow, painful walk to the hospital entrance with Jane by my side. I was glad we were pretty close to the doors.

I didn't speak until we stopped walking. I could hardly breathe and was worried I was going to pass out.

"Okay, Zack. I should get going. I guess I'll see you around? You'll probably be away from school for a while, right?" Jane said, as she shuffled her feet around.

"He'll be out a couple of days, probably," my mom answered for me, as she came up the walk to help me to the car.

"Can I call you?" I asked Jane.

She shook her head back and forth, looking mortified. We all started a slow shuffle to Mom's car.

"Uh, I mean, I'll see you at school in a couple of days. Or maybe if you need anything, I could . . . ."

She avoided my eyes. She was shy. I loved it.

"I guess you could call," Jane said and looked at my mom and then back at me. "I mean, if you need anything picked up from school or something—" She directed the message to my mom, but she really was talking to me.

"Thanks." My mom opened the passenger door for me. "Bye, Jane."

"Thanks," I added. "See ya soon?"

"Bye." Jane practically ran away from us, towards the parking lot and the sanctuary of her own car.

I slid into the seat of Mom's car as carefully as I could manage.

Mom got into the driver's seat. "Let me do up your seatbelt." She reached over and pulled the strap across my chest. I winced a little. "Sorry, babe, but we have to put this on."

I nodded and she clicked the seatbelt into place before starting up the car.

"That was nice of her to come. She's a good friend?" Mom asked as she shoulder checked and pulled out of the parking spot. She didn't look at me.

"Yeah. Maybe more." I said it softly. Hopefully, I added silently to myself.

"Really? I still don't think she seems like your type." Her voice tinged with disapproval.

"What's my type, Mom?" I turned to glare at her as she pulled out into traffic.

"I don't know. I just see you with someone more like Claire."

I gritted my teeth, in both anger and pain. "You know what, Mom? Claire is very over."

"I know. And you miss her. I understand that. But, you don't have to go out with the first girl to pay attention to you." She watched the road.

I shook my head. "Mom. Stop it. You don't understand anything, okay? I don't miss Claire. And Jane is not the first girl to pay attention to me. She happens to be the first girl that I like. And no, she's nothing like Claire. Believe me, that's a good thing." I turned from her and, looking out the window, could see Jane's car coming up behind us.

My mom glanced at me. "What really happened with Claire?"

"Nothing, Mom. I don't want to talk about it."

She pressed her lips together. I could tell she was working hard at not asking any more questions.

"So, this Jane . . . she's a nice girl?"

"Yes."

"It's just that her makeup, she dresses so . . . and she looks so . . . ."

"So *what*?"

"I don't know. What do you kids call it? Goth? Punk? I just don't think she's your type."

"My type again. Forget it, Mom. I like her. Her appearance is not what it seems."

"Meaning?"

"She's awesome."

My mom glanced at me again, but wisely kept her mouth shut this time.

We drove in silence down the highway and back to town. It was dark. I hoped Jane wasn't scared, but I didn't imagine she would be. She didn't seem like she'd frighten easily.

"This is going to keep you out of commission for a couple of weeks. Luckily, you should be back playing hockey by the time the scouts are around. God, I hope so. I could kill that kid! This is such an important year for you." Mom was again refocused on what she saw as the most important thing in my life.

I shrugged and gazed out the window at the blackness. I tuned out my mother's comments on scouts and what they would expect from me after an injury like mine.

Her obsession with my hockey suddenly seemed bizarre. There she was, a quasi-intellectual and all, and she wanted nothing more than for me to play a game for a living. It hadn't worked out so well for her—the hockey wife gig, I mean—yet it was still so important to her that I turn pro.

Secretly, I was kind of glad to be forced off the ice for a couple of weeks. It would give me time to concentrate on other interests, like Jane.

I glanced at my mom and smiled. She reached over and patted my leg, misunderstanding the source of my smile.

"It'll work out, Zachary. Don't worry."

"I know, Mom."

But we were talking about completely different things.

CHAPTER

8

"Zachary Chase. As I live and breathe! So the rumors were true. You have blessed us with your presence at our first meeting for the school musical."

So much for sneaking in unnoticed; Mr. Wright busted me on my first footstep into the drama room.

It was only a few weeks after that drive home from the hospital, and Mr. Wright grinned at me as I walked into his classroom. I was late, but I just shrugged at Mr. Wright, feeling all of the eyes in the room as they followed me. Some were friendly, some were not. It didn't matter so much, as I sought out the one pair of eyes that counted: Jane's. She smiled at me from beside Cassandra. I walked close to where they sat, and leaned against the wall.

Sheila sat close to them, too. I lifted my hand to wave. She already knew about my plan to show up. She waved back.

"Sorry I'm late," I said to Mr. Wright, who by now had stopped talking.

"This meeting is for the school musical," he said, sounding amused.

"I know." I ignored the laughter.

I thought I saw a look of pleasure on his face, but it disappeared as quickly as it emerged.

"Sit down, Zachary," he told me.

"If you don't mind, I'll stand. It still hurts when I sit for too long."

He glanced at my stomach as if looking for evidence, then nodded, turning his attention back to the room.

I looked right at Jane.

"Hi," I mouthed.

I noticed her eyes were a little less heavily made up. She wore a short T-shirt that looked like she'd hacked it up with a pair of scissors, with a long white one underneath. I glanced down and saw she was wearing a short skirt, with black fishnet stockings and high-cut black Converse shoes. I grinned at her, in my faded Abercrombie jeans and baggy T-shirt. We looked like an odd couple together. I liked that—surprises.

Cassandra shot me a look. Her eyes weren't unfriendly, but she looked around cautiously before rewarding me with a tiny grin. She still didn't trust me. And I bet she'd been burnt a lot in the past because of her size.

I winked at her, and smiled when she quickly turned her head away.

"Okay, Mr. Chase?" Mr. Wright's voice cut into my thoughts.

I glanced at him, no idea what he'd just said. A few of the kids giggled. I spotted Mona sitting off to the side of the class. She watched me, a sad smile on her face. I nodded her way.

"Sorry?" I said turning my attention back to Mr. Wright.

"I asked if you'd help me collect names."

"Sure." I pushed myself off the wall I'd been leaning on.

"Okay, kids. Line up. Leads in one line, extras in the other. Zachary, come here and take this clipboard. Extras, line up over here by Zachary. Just write down their names, okay, Zack?"

I reached Mr. Wright at the front of the room. "You trying out for a lead or an extra?" he asked me.

I shrugged. "An extra, I guess."

He grinned. "You don't want to go out for the lead?"

I raised my eyebrows. "Not this time. Sore ribs."

"You can sing?"

"I dabble. When I'm playing guitar."

He smiled as he shook his head. "Okay, son. I'll put you to good use." He held out a clipboard. "Here, take this and go stand over there. Write down the names of all the kids who want to be extras."

Sheila was the first person in line.

"Zack Chase. The singing hockey player. You going to sing in front of the whole school? You are the weirdest guy."

"That so?" I tapped a pencil against the clipboard. I got sick of being called weird all the time. Seemed to me, I wasn't even close to being the wackiest character in this town.

She nodded, then glanced towards the back of the line where Jane stood. Cassandra was across the room, in the lead parts' line, looking both flustered and nervous.

"Well," I said, "you've never heard me sing. Maybe I'll surprise you. And by the way, you're a very weird girl, too, Sheila. And that's exactly why you like me."

She stuck her tongue out as I wrote her name on the first line.

"Sheila Hannigan. Extra. Sure you don't want to go for something with a little bit more bite, Sheila? You've got enough drama queen in you to take on something a little meatier."

"Ha. Ha. You better not be referring to the size of my butt." She glanced meaningfully back at Jane. "This how you get the girl? By landing a part in the school play?"

I didn't answer; instead I just shot her my cockiest smile.

"A singing hockey player. Lord have mercy." She rolled her eyes, then leaned forward, touching my arm. "Hey. I miss you. I hardly see you anymore. I can't believe you haven't been at the rink watching the games. Coach Cal has got to be pissed off. It doesn't look so good if you don't at least show an interest in the team when you're down for the count."

I leaned forward so only Sheila could hear me. "Screw how it looks." I leaned back.

"Ribs still hurt. It's hard to sit in one spot for long. I'm just taking it easy right now." It was my official answer, the same one I'd been giving my mom for the last couple of weeks. She was starting to fret about my not supporting the team and not going to the games, but I still refused to go.

Sheila seemed ready to launch into a further lecture, but I'd heard enough of it at home, so I just tuned her out.

"Okay, Sheila. I have to get everyone signed up. Do you mind moving along?" She reluctantly left my side.

I signed up a couple more kids, and then Mona appeared at the front of the line.

"Hey, Mona," I smiled at her. "You're an extra, too."

"Zack." She blushed. "Um, hi." She didn't look me in the eye.

"I didn't know you were into acting."

She glanced around as if someone were going to materialize to give her trouble. "Well. I used to be. I haven't done anything for a long time, but I thought I might try out. You know, just as an extra. See if I still like it."

I nodded. "Cool."

"You're trying out, too?"

I nodded again. "What the hell. I might as well, since I can't play hockey for a couple more weeks."

She actually looked like she cared. I couldn't figure this girl out at all. One minute she was a trash-talking nympho, and the next she was blushing and sad, and trying out for the school musical.

"You going to wear your Hawaiian lei as the extra?" I teased.

Her eyes widened, her mouth twitched in the corner. "What?"

"Your costume, from Halloween."

"You were at that party?" She looked like she might cry now.

"Uh, yeah." I found it odd, considering her behavior with me at the party.

"I was really drunk." She stared at the floor, and then looked around for an escape. "The whole thing's kind of a blur."

She'd been drunker than I'd even thought if she couldn't remember what happened. Maybe she was pretending not to know—some kind of pride or something.

"Oh well, that happens, I guess." I couldn't think of anything else to say.

"Yeah. To me. Are your ribs still sore?" she asked in a voice barely above a whisper.

She was changing the topic. I could go along with that. "Nah. They're fine. I'm getting better. So, is Candy going to try out, too?"

"Oh my God, no way. She's going to freak when she finds out I did." She looked around again. Was she expecting to be pulled out of line and scolded?

"Well. Good for you then, doing your own thing."

She smiled and it reached her eyes this time.

"Yeah. Good for me."

I wrote down her name. "What's your last name, Mona?"

"Ryder."

"I guess I don't get one?" I winked.

She stared at me with a blank look.

"A ride?"

A laugh spilled out of her. She brought her hand up to cover her mouth, as if it surprised her. For a moment I could see what she'd been like when she was younger. Innocent, cute.

"See ya around, Mona Ryder."

"See you, Zack." She looked about to step away, and then glanced at the line behind her and back at me again. "You going out with Jane?"

I shrugged. "I'm trying."

She nodded. "I thought so. She's a nice girl."

She walked away and I glanced at the next girl in line, but glimpsed back to the end of the line. Jane watched Mona walk out. The sad look on Jane's face confused me.

I quickly signed up the rest of the people in line without additional chitchat, until Jane stood before me.

"I won't put your name on this list until you agree to go out with me."

She bit her lower lip.

"Okay," she said.

Score!

CHAPTER 9

"You look amazing, Jane."

Finally, the day I'd been looking forward to arrived.

"Please." She rolled her eyes, but then she smiled at me. Her teeth were small. She didn't have an overly large mouth or big swollen lips like a lot of girls. The tiny mouth suited her.

She wore a simple pair of jeans that made her butt look incredible, along with a snug black T-shirt with a skull on the front. She wore big black army boots, and her hair was pulled back into a simple ponytail. She'd traced her eyes with black eyeliner, but it was a little tamer than before. To me, she looked beautiful. She even smelled delicious; she was wearing a light perfume and the scent was somehow familiar.

"I hope you weren't expecting me to transform into Barbie."

"Hardly. You look great, like Avril Lavigne."

"Oh, God." She rolled her eyes again.

"Not a compliment?" I reached down to try and take her hand.

She pulled away and shook her head. "You look like somebody famous, but I can't decide who," she said, with her brow furrowed.

I lifted her hand and lightly put my lips to her fingers. She blushed intensely and pulled away again.

"Flattery will get you everywhere, Ms. Parker." I grinned.

She laughed, and the sound made me want her to do it again.

"So. I thought I would take you out for dinner. Is that okay?" I asked as we strolled down the driveway together.

"I like to eat."

I raised a brow. "Hmm. I wouldn't have guessed. I don't know where you put it."

"Very funny."

"Hey. You're lucky. Most girls would kill to look like you."

She made a groaning sound, and I decided to let up.

"Do you mind walking? I thought we would go to Western Pizza. Is that okay? It's not very far."

"You don't have your license yet, do you?"

I grinned. "Busted. Late birthday. I could always call my mom to drive us if you don't want to walk."

"No—I love to walk," she said quickly.

We headed down the path from her house to the street, strolling in the warm evening air and keeping our conversation light. We argued and teased as we put our feelers out, trying to know each other a little at a time.

We reached the pizza place in fifteen minutes and were seated at a tiny table for two. The place was old, with cheap plastic tablecloths, but I'd heard the food was great. We easily agreed on the same kind of pizza, and when it arrived we dug in with gusto.

"So, what made you want to be in the school play, Zack Attack?" Jane asked, with a bite of pizza in her mouth.

"Truthfully?"

She was adorable, chomping on that pizza like she meant it. She wasn't shy around food. That was interesting.

She nodded.

"You," I said, balancing my slice of ham and pineapple pizza in the air in front of my mouth.

"Get out," she said, ripping a chunk off the slice she held in her hand.

I watched her chew and she stared back at me, shameless in her gluttony. It made me like her even more. I bit my own slice, chewed, and then smiled.

"Well. Okay. I signed up because I wanted to talk to you, but you know what? I actually like it. I like the rehearsals and seeing how the whole thing comes together. It makes sense to me now, why people get involved behind the scenes and in smaller roles. Everybody has something they're good at, right? I mean, everyone pitches in. The stars of the show get to shine more than the others, but it doesn't make them better or more important. I always thought being the star was the most important thing. But now I see that everyone works together. It's kind of like preparing for the playoffs. I've learned a lot in the show.

Besides, it's a cool story. Bad boy, good girl. Kind of like me and you." I winked at her and took another big bite of pizza.

"Ha, ha." She grinned at me. "You are *so* not a bad boy."

I tilted my head to stare her down. "Yes, but are you a good girl?"

She blushed down at the red-checkered tablecloth. Then she looked up at me, and it was all I could do not to lunge across the table and kiss her. Ms. Parker was not all she appeared to be.

Jane changed the subject to Cassandra, and for a while we talked about how talented she was. When the waiter came to clear our plates, Jane's face suddenly grew serious.

"Did you hear about Candy's party tonight?" she asked.

"Who didn't? Her parents are in the Caribbean and she's throwing a gigantic bash."

"Yeah. She's crazy. And I'm sure she'll get caught." She took a deep breath. "Would you mind if we stopped by for a while? I know it'll suck, but I told my parents I'd go and keep an eye on David. I promised him I would, and it's the only way they'd let him go. We could walk back to my place and take my car to the party."

"You his keeper?" I asked. I put down some money for the waiter.

"No." She studied my face for a moment. "They're worried about him. About his drinking."

"David?" I thought about the conversation I'd had with him, but didn't say anything to Jane.

"He's drinking way too much. It's getting him into trouble. And they don't know how to handle it. Their solution's using me as a chaperone." She pointed to the check. "What do I owe you?"

I put up my hand and waved her off. "Nothing. It's my treat. That's some kind of pressure for you, having to look after David."

"Not really. He's a jerk, but he's my twin. I'm worried about him, too, but what can I do? I mean, I can't tell him not to drink. He's not going to listen to me. Are you sure you got this tab?"

I nodded. "You're right—he probably wouldn't listen to you. And since I asked you out to dinner, I pay."

"Thanks." She smiled. "I really hate these parties, you know. All those people getting drunk and doing stupid things." She shook her head, and then blinked at me. "How come you don't drink?" she asked me.

"I drink. I just don't get drunk. I mean, I have. Gotten drunk. Thrown up, the whole nine yards. But I don't like it. I don't like losing control." I traced the pattern on the table with my fingertips, then I looked up.

She nodded. "Me neither."

I decided to take the chance. "Plus, you know, my dad."

She didn't say anything, but her features softened and she leaned forward to listen.

"Everyone seems to know how he died. He was drunk. On the road for a game. My mom was at home, pregnant with me, and he went out drinking after the game with two of his hockey buddies. A couple of girls were in the back seat. They all died in the crash." I shook my head. "I can't believe he would do something like that to my mom."

Jane reached across the table and stroked my hand. "It doesn't mean anything. The girls in the back, I mean. He was probably just giving them a ride or something. He was with other guys, too."

I loved the feel of her fingers on my hand. "That's what my mom believes. She believes it absolutely—with her whole heart. She told me he would never fool around on her. She's so sure. She loved him a lot. Me, I'm not so sure. I think he was fooling around."

"She told you all that?"

I smiled and nodded. "She talks to me about everything." I frowned a little. Well she had—until Jane.

"You and your mom are close." It wasn't a question.

"Well, yeah. I mean, we've moved around a lot, so we rely on each other. She was really ambitious for so many years. Moving for promotions and new territories. Then this year, she just kind of stopped running so fast. It was like she'd been trying to get away from her memories or something. And she's finally done. She quit her job and I think she's happier now. Her sister is here. She likes Hale-town, and I think she's ready to settle. Plus, she thinks I'm going to get drafted from here. So many good junior teams. She wants me to play pro hockey, like my dad." I shrugged, pulled my hand back.

"You don't want to?"

"I don't know. I can't figure it out. I'm not sure if it's just her dreams for me or if it's what I want."

"You're not like most hockey players, Zachary."

"That's what everyone tells me. I just want to be me, you know. I don't want to be my dad. I don't want to live his life. I want to live my own . . . ." I shrugged and got up from the table, holding out my hand to help her up. "I'm just not sure I know how."

"I totally get it," she said and accepted my help without a fuss.

Her fingers reached up and traced my scar.

"You've been hurt," she said, then dropped her fingers to her side.

"So have you." I stood straighter, smiling at her like a love-struck goofball.

She smiled back. "You want to go to a party?" she asked.

"Not really."

"Me either. But duty calls. So can we go?"

"Of course."

My insides were doing a happy dance as we walked back to her house. The night was warm and the air clean and fresh.

"I think I like living here," I told Jane.

"I'm glad. I think I like you living here, too."

"You know how I feel right now?"

I let go of her hand for a moment and did a cartwheel on the road in front of her. "That's how I feel."

Ouch. I didn't tell her how much that hurt my ribs.

She put her hands over her mouth and giggled. She laughed and laughed, and it was the most adorable sound

I'd ever heard. I put my arm around her and we walked back to her house.

We could hear music and sounds of the party as soon as Jane turned off the ignition. The entire block was jammed with cars. We parked at the end of the street.

I jumped out of Jane's car when she parked, then went around to open her door.

"You freak me out when you do that."

I laughed. "Sorry. My mom beat it into me."

She stepped out of the car. "I'm not saying I don't like it—it's just not normal."

I reached for her hand and she didn't pull back, that is, until a voice interrupted us and she dropped it right away.

"Looky what we found on our beer run, boys. Isn't this sweet. What a great couple. The pretty boy and my very own bad girl. You closing your eyes and pretending he's me when you go at it, Jane? And you, Chase. You closing your eyes and pretending she's your mommy?"

I didn't have to look behind me to know who the voice belonged to—Mac. I also guessed Cole and Eddie were attached to either side of him.

I turned my head. There they were, right in place.

Jane spoke softly. "Ignore him, Zachary. He's baiting you. I hate his guts and he knows it; he's trying to get you to do something stupid." She put a hand on my arm to hold me back.

I almost shook with the effort of not going after him. My ribs ached a little, as if sensing my thoughts and reminding me they weren't up to it.

"Can't even think of a comeback, Chase? That's so totally lame, dude. The little knock you took on the ice obviously jiggled around more than your ribs. Too chicken to keep playing with the big boys, as far as I can see. Might as well just hand in your uniform now. Season is getting close to playoffs. Scouts'll be sniffing around soon. Can't measure up to the old man, so you decided to take a dive?"

I tore away from Jane and pinned Mac on the ground. He was underneath my knee before he even knew what hit him.

"Zachary! Leave him alone. Leave him alone! He's not worth it." I heard Jane shouting at me, but I focused only on the face on the ground in front of me.

I leaned my head forward and spoke right into his ear. "You are dead if you ever mess with her again, Mac! Ever. And we'll see who makes the cut, won't we? I don't have to lower myself to getting goons to take out my competition. Not that I consider you much of a threat. You're weak, you're stupid, and you have no idea what it takes to be a leader."

I stood up as Cole and Eddie started grabbing at my arms. I shook them off. "Take it easy, guys. Friendly little chat between friends, nothing more."

Mac jumped up, but his buddies held him back. "She's a slut, man. Goth girl gives good head. You know what I mean?"

My blood boiled under my skin. I imagined it bubbling with rage, just like the Incredible Hulk.

"Forget it, Zack. Let's just go inside, please." Jane pulled on my arm and didn't even look at Mac.

I allowed her to pull me away, itching to go after Mac, but letting my head win out for once. Jane wouldn't be happy if I fought with Mac on our date.

I called out: "Listen. Cole, Eddie. We're only here to check out the party for a while. Why don't you guys take your time buying beer, cool him down, and we'll all act like civilized human beings inside. We'll be out of your way shortly, and then you guys can carry on doing whatever it is you do at parties."

I continued walking at Jane's side, ignoring Mac's cursing. I took her hand and we walked towards Candy's house.

"He better stay away from you." I mumbled under my breath. I thought of Jane's voice coming from the bathroom and how scared she'd sounded. The thought of Mac's hands on her made me crazy; I put my arm around her. "Why's he so pissed at you anyway, Jane?"

She tried to pull away from me. But I held on.

"Zachary, let me go. Trust me, you're just making him madder."

I kept walking until I'd put some distance between us and the three boys in the street.

"They're assholes, Jane. Forget about it."

She stopped. "I already have. You forget about it, too. He's saying things to piss you off. Forget about it and just be careful, okay? You have no idea what Mac is capable of."

I shook my head. "No. I know exactly what he's capable of. What he doesn't know is what *I'm* capable of."

She reached up and pushed a stray strand of hair out of my eyes. "You're almost scaring me."

I smiled. "I'm on your side. There's nothing to be afraid of."

"No! I mean it. He's not worth it. Forget about him. You can kick his ass once you get back on the ice, and he knows it. You're totally freaking him out. He's not good at losing, and he's just a stupid little boy trying to impress his daddy. And his dad, well, he's not a nice man. And he's not handling very well having someone on the ice who's better than Mac. Mac is just trying to rattle you, to throw you off. He only wants to shake you so he can be the best. Just forget about him."

"Not going to happen."

She studied my face for a moment. She forced a smile. "No. I guess not." She looked away. She met my eyes again. "Come on. Let's go find David so we can get the hell out of here."

"Deal." I wanted nothing more than to get her out of that house, away from Mac, and alone with me again.

We went up the front walk to Candy's house. Like most of the people in Haletown, her parents were obviously doing okay for themselves. The huge house had a three-car garage and expensive landscaping. Even I could tell a lot of money had been spent on it. But now, empty bottles of beer littered the front lawn and elaborate flowerbeds. Someone wasn't going to be happy with Candy once this party was over.

We stepped inside the house. The front hallway was crammed with people. The air inside was smoky and hot. Music blasted from an expensive stereo system with built-in speakers all through the house. Kids sipped bottles of beer and wine coolers, lounging anywhere there was an empty space.

We squeezed through the crowd of people. I recognized kids from school, but there were also a lot I didn't know. It looked like every kid in town and beyond it had shown up for this party.

As we maneuvered around bodies, I spotted Mona sitting on the stairs. Judging by her slack features and glassy eyes, she already was completely wasted. I looked back as Jane and I got separated in the throng of people. I nodded my head towards the staircase and she nodded back, trying to squeeze her way through them and back to me.

I walked over to Mona and bent down to talk to her. I put my hand on her shoulder.

"Hey, Mona. What's up?"

She lifted her head and tried to focus with her droopy wandering eyes.

"Zacky," she slurred. "God, you're so cute." She giggled a little and then hiccupped. Her head bobbled unsteadily.

She tried to stand and I steadied her. She wrapped an arm around my neck. "You want a blow job?" she asked.

I shook my head and gave her a wry smile.

"Mona. Don't talk to me like that, okay? You need a friend, and I can be one, you know." It seemed to me like the girl truly was in need of one.

She leaned against me. "Bullshit. You're just like the rest of them. You just want to screw me and that's it. I don't have any friends. Especially male ones." She sounded drunk but sad. Or maybe she was defeated. Angry.

"Is everything okay?" Jane reached my side and looked at Mona with pity in her eyes.

"She's drunk," I told her.

Jane nodded. It was pretty obvious, I guess.

Mona sighed dramatically. "Not drunk. Tired." Her eyes focused on Jane. "Oh. It's you." She sighed heavily again. "You stole Zack from me. And you're *so* not his type."

I shook my head at Jane to tell her not to respond. Mona was almost totally out of it.

Jane nodded, understanding.

"Do you want us to take you upstairs, to Candy's room? So you can lie down for a while?" Jane asked.

Mona nodded again. Jane took Mona by the arm.

"Come on, Mona. I still remember where her room is. You're probably sleeping over at Candy's tonight, right?"

Mona made some gurgling noises. I went to her other side, supporting her as we made our way up the stairs. We scooted past couples making out and heard a few laughs and whistles in Mona's direction. Candy's room was off the main part of the house, tucked in a back hallway off a room that looked like it was used as an office. Luckily no kids had migrated to this part of the house—yet.

"It's over there," Jane said, pointing to a closed door.

Between the two of us, we managed to get Mona into

the bedroom. I would have laughed when I opened the door if we weren't escorting such a drunk, messed-up girl. Candy's room was exactly as I would have imagined it. Pink. Frilly. Posters of movie stars on her walls. Ribbons she'd won. Lots of pictures of herself at various stages in her life.

We eased Mona onto Candy's pink bed and she got under the comforter, her eyes closed and mumbling.

"You think she'll be all right?" I asked Jane.

"She might throw up all over Candy's pink sheets, but other than that, she probably just needs to sleep it off."

I nodded.

We left, closing the door behind us.

"How do you know where Candy's room is, anyway?" I asked.

"Zachary, I've lived in this town since I was a kid. I've been to her house before. I hung out with her a couple times when we were younger. With Mona."

That floored me. I wanted to ask more, but she tugged my arm and hurried us back down the hallway towards the stairs.

"Now we have to find Drunk Number Two," Jane said.

This time, she pulled me through the crowd, leading me down a crowded hallway, past a luxurious dining room and into the kitchen.

"What the hell?" Jane asked. I looked over to see what she was looking at.

Candy leaned against the counter, her arms wrapped around a husky guy, her tongue practically down his throat. But he wasn't David.

"Candy! Candy!" Jane rushed towards them. "Where's David?"

Candy unwrapped herself from the big guy and gave Jane a bored, bitchy look.

"I have no idea. Last time I saw him he was puking all over my mother's rose bushes."

"Where is he now?"

Candy didn't answer, she'd already returned to her make-out session.

"Shit." Jane said as she hurried out of the kitchen and down another hallway.

"This is a freaking huge house," I mumbled as I followed her.

She moved quickly, reaching a door at the back of the house, then yanking it open. I followed her to the back yard.

It was gigantic. Kids hung out all over a huge wrap-around deck, and there was still an expansive amount of property beyond it, almost like a fancy park. It featured huge rocks and more landscaping. Someone paid a pretty penny for a spread like that.

"David!" Jane called into the air.

A few kids looked over at us. "You looking for your brother?" asked a preppy-looking girl in a tight dress.

Jane nodded.

The girl pointed out into the vast yard. "He was out back there a while ago, puking his guts out."

Jane rushed off the deck into the garden. I followed, a little less enthusiastically. Seeing David puking his guts out wasn't one of the sights I'd hoped for on my date with Jane.

"David!" she shouted.

"He's over here," called a female voice.

I ran behind Jane to the source of the voice, recognizing it immediately.

I worked at not smiling when I saw them. Sheila sat on a stone bench in front of a pond, her curly red hair framing her face. Beside her, in the fetal position lay David, with his head in her lap. She was holding his hand.

"He's been really sick," she whispered. "He passed out a while ago, so I thought I'd let him, you know, stay asleep for a while. I've been wondering how I was going to get him out of here, and how to sober him up a bit before he has to go home."

Jane and I moved closer to them. David was lying on his side, his mouth open, and almost snoring as he breathed in and out. I turned my head at the very foul smell of him.

I looked down at Sheila. She shrugged. "He scared me, you know? He was so sick. I was going to call someone, but then he just started, I don't know, almost like crying a little, and then he crawled into my lap like this." Her eyes darted around the yard.

"He stinks," I said.

Jane gave me a dirty look before reaching down to shake her brother's shoulder.

Sheila ignored me. "I was really worried about him," she told Jane. "I've never seen anyone so drunk before."

"David . . . David! Wake up!" Jane shook him again.

He groaned, and then his head rolled off of Sheila's lap and smacked into the stone bench.

"Owww," he moaned. He didn't open his eyes.

Sheila raised his head, placing it again on her lap and off the hard stone.

"What happened?" Jane asked her.

Sheila shook her curls. I could almost feel her anger burning.

"It was that bitch, Candy."

"I knew she was involved." Jane stiffened beside me.

"Some guy showed up from out of town, looking for Candy." Jane and I nodded. We'd both seen her with him in the kitchen.

"Candy was flirting with him and David was getting pissed off. So she started taunting him, making him do more and more shooters to 'please' her. I think it was tequila."

I winced on David's behalf. As if sensing our conversation, he picked up his head again, then hurled all over the ground in front of him.

Jane and I took a quick step back and out of the way.

"Nasty," I said.

"Nice choice of girlfriends," Sheila added, picking up her feet and checking them for vomit. David dropped his head back into her lap.

Jane stepped forward again. "David. . .David! You're going to have to wake up." She shook him again. "Ugh! He smells so gross."

But David didn't move.

I shook my head. I must really like this girl a lot to do what I was about to do.

"I'll help him up," I volunteered.

The look on Jane's face was thanks enough.

I bent over him. "Okay, Parker, I'm going to help you up now." I slid my hands under David's arms.

"I sure as hell hope he used deodorant."

Sheila gave me a disgusted look.

I blew out some air. "You're right, he smells bad enough as it is. Deodorant wouldn't help."

I tried to avoid stepping in the gross-looking vomit but it was unavoidable. I shook my head and bent down to haul him up, then yelled in pain. Everything went black for a moment.

"Oh, Zack. Your ribs!" Jane cried.

"Come on," said Sheila.

The girls came up on either side of me and tried to lift him. But David was dead weight and very heavy. Then, all three of them crumpled to the ground.

I helped Jane and Sheila to get up, but we left David lying on the grass.

"Shit. I'll go get someone to help us." I felt like such a wimp, not able to even lift David myself, let alone carry him out.

I took off running towards the deck. Searching around, I tried to spot some strong-looking guys to help us move David to Jane's car.

"Dude, can you give me a hand?" I called to the biggest kid on the deck. I recognized him from school but I didn't know his name.

He glanced at me, questioningly.

"What's up?" he said.

"We need to carry David Parker out of here. He passed out."

"Forget it, dude. I saw him puking. That's nasty. Go get one of your hockey bros to do your dirty work instead."

I sighed. I understood his sentiments in more ways than one.

I sped up the steps and went inside the house. Running down the hallway, I looked for someone else who could help us.

Out of the corner of one eye, I spotted Mac and his sidekicks. They were on the stairs, laughing and teasing a couple of girls. Mac glanced up and spotted me. Then his face went blank. I could see the hate in his expression. I shook my head and turned the other way, and walked into the kitchen. I looked around the crowded room. Candy and her boy-toy were gone. Then I spotted a couple of teammates with some girls.

"Smith, Coop. Can you guys give me a hand? Parker passed out in the garden and I need help carrying him out of here." I pointed at my ribs. "I can't do it myself."

Danny Smith glanced over and nodded, putting his beer down and kissing his girl on the cheek. He walked towards me, with Cooper following.

"What's Parker done now?"

"Tequila shooters," I answered.

They laughed and shook their heads, following me outside.

When we got to David, they both grunted in disgust.

"Man, that is so seriously rancid."

"I know. Come on, let's get him up and out of here," I replied with my own grimace.

"There's a gate over there," Sheila said, pointing to the side of the house. "We can take him out that way to Jane's car instead of dragging him back through the house."

I helped the guys to maneuver Parker up as best I could. They dropped him and picked him up a couple times when he made coughing sounds like he was going to barf all over again.

"He's so out of it." Jane sounded truly afraid.

The guys helped get him out of the yard, but it took at least ten minutes to take him the full block to Jane's car. He was heavy. They propped him up against the car for a rest, before trying to get him inside.

Jane and Sheila waited, not saying much. They both were quiet and worried about David.

I looked at Smith and Coop. "You'll help me get David inside the car?" I asked.

"You totally owe us," Smith said.

I nodded. I went to Jane and leaned down to speak into her ear so only she could hear what I was saying.

"I'm going to just run upstairs and check on Mona before we take off. I want to make sure she's going to be okay."

Jane stared at me with big eyes. "Zachary. You're sweet to worry about Mona."

"No, I'm not," I told her. "Anyhow, she's an okay girl, Jane. She's really sad, and just trying to figure out how to fit into this messed-up world of ours." I looked around at all of us. We were all trying to do the same thing in our own way.

Jane nodded. "Okay. Hurry back. I need to get David into the house before my parents get home."

"Sheila? You'll stay with Jane?" I asked.

Sheila nodded. "Where're you going?"

"Just to check on a friend."

I took off for the front door, maneuvering my way through the partiers and bolting up the stairs two at a time.

I ran down the hallway to the room where we'd left Mona, slowing down as I approached the door. I turned the knob, pushing the door open to see where we'd left Mona.

Then I erupted with a bellow of rage.

Mac was on top of Mona. He was half naked and he was having sex with her. They both turned to look towards the door. Mona's eyes were fuzzy; she was out of it, confused.

"Zack?" she said, looking up at Mac on top of her. "What's going on?"

Mac jumped off of her, grabbing his pants from the bed and holding them in front of him. He hadn't even bothered to take off his shirt.

"Get out of here, Chase. This is a private party. You're not invited. Why don't you go and screw Parker's dyke of a sister."

Mona began to cry. "It's okay. He always has sex with me when I'm drunk." She snorted, hiccupping. She sounded close to hysteria.

I shook my head. "Mac! Get the hell out of here and leave her alone! She's so wasted, she doesn't even know what the hell's going on. This is wrong, Mac. You should never have sex with a girl who's drunk. You understand me? Never!" I was livid, but at the same time I felt so sorry and embarrassed for Mona. I went to the bed and pulled the covers up over her, then turned to Mac who was still hopping around, pulling on his pants.

"You ever come near her again, I'll tear you apart, limb by limb. You understand me?" I shouted.

"Just 'cause you're not gettin' any yourself doesn't mean you have to interrupt someone else who's gettin' some. Good luck getting any outta Jane. She's only got eyes for me."

He took off out of the door before I could do anything else. My ribs still ached from trying to lift David, and I was a little thankful Mac was gone.

I turned back to the bed. Mona rolled over and turned away from me, facing the wall. Her shoulders were shaking.

"Mona?"

She didn't answer.

"Mona. Can we take you home?"

"Go away. Just get out of here, Zack."

I touched her back and she scooted as far away from me as she could get, until she was against the wall.

"Get out! Just get out!" she shouted.

I stood in place, watching her cry, not knowing what to do.

"Don't let anyone else come in here," I said.

I went to the door and checked it. It had a lock. "I'm going to lock the door behind me, so no one else can get in. Okay?"

"Just *go*!" she screamed.

I crept out, locking the door behind me. I stood in the hallway for a moment, unsure of what else to do. Then I shrugged, shook my head and left.

CHAPTER

10

Jane, Sheila, and I stood in the upstairs hallway of Jane's house, panting. The three of us had somehow managed to get David out of Jane's car and into his bed.

I heard sounds coming from downstairs. I glanced at Jane.

"Oh, no!" she said softly. "They're home. Come on."

She led us back down the stairs. Her parents looked up from the hallway, a little startled to see the three of us coming downstairs and into the living room.

I saw her dad glance at his watch. Then I snuck a look at my own. It was already past midnight. My stomach did some flip-flopping. I wasn't very good with fathers. In fact, I hated talking to them.

"It's late. What's going on, Jane?" Her father asked.

"This is Sheila, and this is Zachary. Um, they were helping me with David."

Her mom walked towards the stairs. "What's wrong with David?"

Nobody said anything.

"Zack from hockey?" Jane's dad asked, scrutinizing

me. For some reason, he didn't seem very happy to see me.

I glanced at her mom, and then forced myself to turn back to her dad; I looked right into his eyes. I hadn't done anything inappropriate.

"What's wrong with David? What have you kids been doing to him? Where's Candy?" her mom asked, her voice rising and beginning to sound a bit hysterical. She started up the stairs, still looking over her shoulder at us.

"He's drunk, Mom. We haven't done anything to him, except move his half-dead carcass across town." Jane sounded angry. "He's totally drunk. He passed out at Candy's party. By the time I got there, he'd already thrown up. You need to thank Sheila for taking care of him. His precious Candy took off with another guy. He might have choked on his own vomit if Sheila hadn't stayed with him."

Her mother glanced at Sheila, half moaned and half cried, then bounded up the stairs, disappearing into David's room.

Jane's father stared at her. "Jane, we're very disappointed in you."

"In me? I'm not the one who got drunk! I'm never the one who gets drunk! This is *not* my fault!" Jane seemed seconds away from stamping her feet. And I didn't blame her, either. I was about to stamp my own in sympathy.

She started pacing, worked up. "It's like you expect David to drink, and you expect me to take care of him. Well, I can't do it every second. Did it ever occur to you that maybe I'd even like a life of my own? When are you going to wake up and face the fact that your precious

David has a serious drinking problem instead of trying to blame me all the time? I have news for you: I'm not going to cover for him anymore. He scared the shit out of me tonight! I almost took him to the hospital. He passed out and could have died. And I can't be there to watch over him 24/7. I'm just his twin, not his bodyguard."

"He doesn't have a drinking problem," her father shouted. "He's a typical teenage boy, and a hockey player!"

"So is Zachary!" Jane shouted. "And *he* doesn't get drunk!"

Mr. Parker glanced at me, but I lowered my eyes and wisely kept my mouth shut for once. I peered down at Sheila, whose expression showed me that she wanted to get the heck out of there as badly as I did.

"He was really sick," Sheila added in a low voice, backing up Jane.

Mr. Parker focused on me again. "Well, why weren't his buddies watching out for him? When I was a kid, that's what we always did. We watched out for each other." Mr. Parker was rapidly losing his cool.

"When *you* were a kid, Grandma and Grandpa watched your hockey games, not your sister. You weren't allowed to be on your own to get drunk all the time, were you?" Jane stared down her father with a withering glare.

"When I was a kid, we lived in a crappy little house and barely had enough money for me to play hockey. I wore second-hand equipment and had to quit before I even got to middle school. Your mother and I both work hard so you kids can have a better life and more than we had." Mr. Parker didn't flinch or look away from her.

"Dad! None of that matters! Are you blind? David's an alcoholic! And it's time you and Mom did something about it. You have to help him. And I can't do it anymore. I can't be responsible for him. I'm not his mother!"

Mr. Parker's features went stiff. Then he trained his glare onto me. I was expecting him to start laying blame on my shoulders when his wife shouted down the stairs.

"Jack! Get up here—now! I can't get David to wake up." Mrs. Parker sounded panicky.

"David's lucky there's no hockey scheduled this weekend. It'd serve him right to play as hung-over as he'll be for the next couple of days." Jane's dad looked at all of us with a frown.

"What difference does it make to you anyway, Dad? You're never at his games to see how he plays," Jane said with a sneer.

Mr. Parker looked at the three of us, considering how to defend his choices. But then Mrs. Parker shouted to him again. Looking nervous and not sure of what to do or say, he turned and darted up the stairs.

Jane watched him go, and then turned to me and Sheila. She lowered her eyes, not meeting our gaze. "I'm sorry," she almost whispered. "Welcome to the Parker family chronicles, where David can do no wrong, and Jane no right." She stared up the stairs after her dad. "We can't keep pretending nothing's wrong much longer."

Sheila half groaned. "Ahh, this is nothing. My mom's on antidepressants, but she still cries all day long. She weighs over 300 pounds and almost never goes out. And my sister's a lesbian, and she's currently coming out in a big way, right here in our conservative little Haletown." Sheila gestured wildly as she spoke.

I nodded. "My dad died drunk, with a carload of groupies he was probably fooling around with. My mom thinks I'm a reincarnation of my dead father. And sometimes I think I am, too."

We all looked at each other. No one laughed.

"We should go," I said softly to Jane.

She nodded. She turned to Sheila, reached out, and touched her arm. "Thanks, Sheila. I don't know what we would have done if you hadn't been there to take care of David."

Sheila shrugged. "It's no big deal. I'm sure someone else would have helped him if I hadn't been around."

Jane shook her head. "I'm not so sure. Anyhow, I don't even want to think about that." She shivered. "Zachary, I'm sorry our night sucked. I wrecked it by dragging you to that stupid party."

"You didn't wreck it, Jane. Up until David puked on my shoes, it was a really great night."

I wanted to kiss her so badly, but her parents were upstairs and Sheila was standing right beside me.

"I had a great time with you, Zack. I'd like to do it again real soon, okay?" She smiled shyly at me and then leaned over and kissed me on the cheek. She flashed a smile at Sheila, and then her mouth formed an O.

"Wait a minute! You're going to need a ride back to Candy's to pick up your car."

"No, it's okay." Sheila said. "I don't want you to get into any more trouble." She glanced towards the stairs.

"I'll walk with you," I said to Sheila. No way I'd let her go back to that party by herself.

"No. Forget it. You guys aren't walking anywhere," Jane said. "I'll just go and tell them I'm driving you back. Wait for me outside, okay?"

Sheila and I walked out.

"She's not bad for a weirdo," Sheila said as the front door closed behind us.

"You're in love with David Parker," I shot back as we headed down the driveway.

"I am not." Sheila's face turned almost purple. "You have no idea what you're talking about."

Jane appeared around the corner in seconds. "Let's go."

"They're okay with you driving us?" I asked.

She shrugged. "They've got their hands full. David was throwing up again. But if I'm not home in ten minutes, they'll go ballistic." She walked to the end of the driveway and clicked open her car door.

"He is so dead!" She didn't smile when she said it. I could tell she was shaken by the whole episode, too.

"He'll be okay," I reassured her as I held the door for her, then climbed into the back seat, letting Sheila sit up front with Jane. "I think he might even want some help now." He needed a lot more help than Jane or I could ever give him.

When we arrived back at the party, the lineup of cars was now a block away from Candy's house. It was getting out of control.

"Where's your car?" Jane asked Sheila.

"Closer to the house. I came early. Don't ask me why."

Jane turned onto Candy's street. Parked in front of Candy's house were a couple of police cars with their lights flashing. Kids were hanging out in front of the house, all chattering and yelling.

"At least the neighbors'll be letting Candy's parents know about the party," I said, smirking. "Maybe she'll be grounded for the rest of her life."

"I doubt it. Her parents don't care," Jane said. "First her sister had the parties, now it's Candy's turn. The cops always show up, but as long as nothing expensive gets broken, she doesn't get into trouble. She's such a Daddy's girl."

I shook my head. People were bizarre; the parents were just as bad as their kids half the time.

"There's my car," Sheila said, pointing to her rust-bucket.

Jane stopped her car beside it. Another car came up behind her and started honking, so Sheila and I leapt out quickly.

"See you, bye, and thanks again," Jane shouted as we hopped out of the car. "See you Monday, Zachary."

I waved as I stretched my legs and watched her drive away.

"Oh, my God, Zachary. You really like her, don't you?" She sounded almost sad.

I didn't look at Sheila. "I don't know. There's something about her. . . ." I glanced at Sheila, but she looked away.

"You make a really weird-looking couple," she said.

I laughed and we hoofed it to her car. She opened my door first, and I was just about to hop inside when I heard someone call my name.

"Chase."

I turned. It was Mac and his two buddies.

"Interrupt me again, faggot, and I'll make you pay." Funny how much tougher he talked with his pals at his side. I thought about Jane's dad's comment about hockey buddies.

I lifted my middle finger. I wasn't going to waste my breath on the guy. What a pig. I'd like to kick his ass, but there wasn't much point in trying. I turned to get into the car.

"Next time, it'll be me on top of Parker's sister," Mac shouted. I turned back just as he laughed and made a rude pumping motion with his hips.

"Oh! Jane," he shouted, making fake sex noises. "Hope she enjoys your ride as much as she does mine. I doubt it, but you can always try her out."

"Zack! Get in the car." Sheila commanded. She pushed me on the shoulder. "Forget him. He's trying to get to you. Get in the damn car!"

I heard Mac laughing. "The only girls this guy can get are loser chicks." By this time, kids from the party were gathering on the front lawn. I felt eyes on my back. I stood up and gently moved Sheila aside.

"I've got to say something, Sheila."

She sighed and stood back.

"You hear what happens to assholes who have sex with girls against their will, Mac?" I said it loud and clear into the night air. "In most places they call it rape. And it doesn't go over real well with the other guys in jail." The buzz and chatter of the watching crowd hushed as quickly as if I'd flipped a switch.

Mac's expression changed. "I don't rape girls to get action." He glanced over at the crowd. My eyes followed his.

"Watch what you're saying," he growled quietly to me.

"Why, Mac? You afraid people might hear the truth?"

Sheila touched my arm. "Zack, be careful."

I shook her off. "No," I said loudly. "I saw him. It's pretty much rape if a girl's too drunk to defend herself, isn't it?" I glanced at the kids watching us, seeing eyes narrow. I lowered my voice. "And it's also wrong to force yourself on girls in bathrooms when they want nothing to do with you."

In the background, I heard comments and catcalls.

"Disgusting creep."

"Typical hockey player."

Mac heard the same remarks and roared with anger. "Mona Ryder's a cheap little slut and everybody knows it. She begged me for it. She wanted it bad."

I gnashed my teeth and rushed at him, talking under my breath. "You keep her name out of it, loser." I shook my head, pissed at myself. Stupid, Zack, stupid. The last thing Mona needed was public humiliation. She had enough problems already. If he mentioned Jane, I'd kill him.

"I left her completely passed out. She wasn't begging for anything—except to be left the hell alone," I said quietly.

I raised my voice then, so others could hear. "You know what, Mac? You're pathetic. You push people around and act tough because inside, you're just a stupid, scared little kid who's trying to prove himself to his daddy. Well, guess what? Daddy won't ever be pleased. Because you'll never be good enough. You're not good enough on the ice, and off the ice, you're a jerk. You're not good enough for any girl in this whole town."

Behind me kids laughed and hooted, especially, from the sounds of it, the non-hockey-playing crowd.

"And guess what? I figured you out the first time I saw you tie up your hockey skates. You're nothing but a selfish creep who's afraid to do anything to upset his daddy."

Mac sputtered and cursed but his friends held him back.

"And just so you know," I added for good measure. "Girls don't like to have sex with guys who force them."

From behind me a girl shouted, "You're a big asshole, Mac. That's disgusting, taking advantage of drunken girls." Her voice wavered as if she'd had too much to drink herself.

Another girl piped up: "I know for a fact you force girls into having sex with you. Or you get them so drunk they can't say no. You're obnoxious and gross. And you probably can't get it any other way."

"Yeah, and your dad's a real psycho, too!" yelled another drunk-sounding guy.

"Screw off, all of you!" Mac shouted at the group of kids and their drunken taunts. Then he turned his wrath on me. "Chase, we'll be talking about this later." He turned to his buddies, waved his hand in the air, and then started walking away. They scurried along behind him.

I wiped my mouth with the back of my hand. "Sheila," I said in a normal voice, "let's get out of here."

She didn't say a word, but zipped around to her side of the car, jumped in, and fired up the ignition.

I climbed into the passenger seat, ignoring the laughter and whoops of the crowd around us. He'd pushed me too far, and he'd gone too far.

"Zack! You are so totally crazy," Sheila said as she drove off. She shook her head. "You just accused him of rape in front of half the school. The other half'll hear about it, word for word, by Monday morning. This is a small town. Oh my God! He's either toast or he's gonna wipe his ass with you."

I shrugged and searched for answers as I stared out the window. My heart pounded and my adrenaline pumped. "Maybe he won't be able to have sex around here for a long, long time."

"Don't kid yourself, Zack. There's always some girl who wants to sleep her way to popularity or else try and change the bad boy." She sighed. "Is it true?" she asked softly. "What he was doing to Mona?"

"Stupid," I muttered. "I shouldn't have brought that up. Mona passed out and it wasn't her fault. I didn't want anyone to find out."

"Well, it's no secret she has sex with a lot of guys. We're talking about Mona Ryder. Everyone knows she's kind of a slut," Sheila said. "I mean, she's okay and all, but she does sleep around. And Mac, well, he has a history with her. And other girls."

"It still doesn't make it okay, Sheila. She was passed out." And then I couldn't help myself. I had to ask.

"Did Jane sleep with him?" I kept my eyes on the window, waiting for her reply. It made me sick to think of Jane with Mac.

Sheila kept her eyes on the road. Shrugged. "I don't know. There're rumors." She glanced at me and grinned. "But the other rumor is that I slept with David Parker. And I'm the only virgin left in Haletown."

I reached for her free hand. "No. You're not the only one."

Sheila pulled up to a red light. She glanced over at me, her eyes wide, then threw back her head, laughing. I looked at her. Her red curls framed her pretty face, and the light shone on her eyes.

"Oh my God, Zack! You totally crack me up." She rubbed my hand with hers, and then leaned forward to slap at my leg. Her boob brushed against my arm.

"You're the most gorgeous boy I've ever met. You're a hockey player. And you're a virgin?"

She looked me in the eyes. Hers sparkled with delight. I grabbed her other hand. She didn't pull away. She smiled, then said, "You're actually still a virgin. Oh, God!"

We stared at each other, kind of giggling, not looking away. Our eyes locked. She was so beautiful, my friend. And fun. And her boobs were enormous. Our smiles faded, but we kept staring at each other. I looked deeply at Sheila, I mean, really looked. She wasn't dark or difficult to get to know. She loved hockey, and for bonus points, she thought I was the most gorgeous guy she'd ever met. I licked my lips.

Suddenly we were all over each other. Kissing, groping.

If you offered me a million dollars for the truth, I honestly couldn't say who made the first move. A car behind us honked. Sheila managed to drive through the green light and pulled over to the side of the road. We kept at it. Kissing, touching. Two mixed-up and hormonally charged virgins, about to make the first and biggest mistake in any male/female best friendship.

CHAPTER

11

"Mom, it's okay. Don't worry about it," I said, quietly.

I knew I shouldn't have told my mom about my fight with Mac, but I was used to telling her mostly everything, and it was a hard habit to break. I didn't give her the full story—just some sketchy details—and I definitely didn't tell her about almost going to bed with my best friend Sheila.

Sheila and I had barely managed to stop ourselves. But at some point, she'd pulled back and convinced me we were being stupid. She'd dropped me off, both of us apologizing profusely, pretending it didn't mean anything and that we'd forget it ever happened. But I didn't sleep very well that night. My hormones were in overdrive again, and I spent a lot of time tossing and turning, not knowing which girl to focus on. I wasn't sure how or what I felt. My head was spinning about the two of them. I definitely had feelings for Jane, without a doubt; but I also totally got into kissing and groping Sheila. It was different. But I didn't want to lose either of them. And I didn't know if I could keep up my friendship with Sheila now. I didn't know what to do, so I stuck close to home and didn't talk to any of my friends for the rest of that weekend.

Mom insisted on driving me to school Monday morning, worried about what Mac was going to do about our fight. She overflowed with unwanted advice on how to handle the situation, and as usual she was fretting about the wrong thing. Mac was the least of my worries. I wasn't the one who took advantage of girls. Or was I? What about what happened with Sheila? And what I'd done with Mona that time at the Halloween party?

"Mac is the captain of your hockey team, so you're going to have to make the first move to apologize. Oh, Zack, I'm so sorry we ever moved here. This place isn't going to help your hockey career at all."

I stared at her profile. "My hockey career? Mom. I'm fifteen. And this isn't about hockey."

She glanced at me, her brows furrowed. "Well, I know. But you need the other players on your side. You said the fight was about a girl who drank too much, wasn't it? And, well, boys will be boys, won't they?"

I stared at her. "You really think drinking's a good excuse? Would you think it was okay if I took advantage of a girl because she was drunk?" I shook my head and turned back to the window. I wanted to say it so badly—that it was my father's job to fool around with drunken groupies, not mine—but I kept quiet.

"Oh, Zack, of course not. But you're not Mac. You'd never take advantage of a girl."

"Wouldn't I?" I glared at her.

She shook her head and gripped the steering wheel. "No, you wouldn't. Come on, this mess doesn't concern you. Remember what's important here. You know what I'm talking about: the NHL. You can't let this little episode stop you from focusing on your dreams. It's all you've ever wanted, just like Jeremy—your father, I mean. I won't allow this horrible boy, this horrible town, to threaten your success."

"Mom! Did it ever occur to you that maybe, just maybe, there're more important things to me than just hockey? I care about other things, too, and other people. I'd like the chance to find out who I am and what I want, instead of just automatically following in my father's footsteps just because I can handle a hockey stick. I want more out of life than that." I stared at her, willing her to see me, instead of him. Trouble was, I'd been acting more like him than I'd ever wanted or expected to.

She did a double take, turning her gaze from the road to me, and then back to the road again. Her facial features drooped. She seemed tired now. "You've always wanted to play hockey. That's all you've ever wanted," she said with a sigh. Her head ping-ponged back and forth again as we pulled up in front of the school. "I mean, I know you can't let people get away with treating others badly, but it's not really your fight, Zack."

"Mom! This is way too deep a conversation for right now. I need to get to class. Don't worry about it. I won't make a big scene. I'll handle it."

She reached out her hand to grab my arm. "Is everything really okay with you? Besides this Mac thing?"

I smiled. "I'm fine, as usual. I'll see ya soon." I opened the door and climbed out.

At the moment, I was a lot more concerned about running into Jane and Sheila than about my hockey future, or even Mac and Mona. I wondered what Jane's parents did to punish her and David. I didn't know what to do. And I wouldn't take any bets about whether Sheila and I had ruined our friendship forever.

I waved Mom off, otherwise she might have sat there forever, waiting to see what would happen. I flung my backpack over my shoulder and headed for the school's front doors. I hoped I didn't run into Sheila first thing.

Groups of girls and some guys were standing around in pairs or threes, hugging each other on the steps outside the doors. I saw a couple of girls wiping tears from their eyes. No one looked my way, or even rushed over to ask for the scoop on Mac. I kept walking towards the front steps, but slowed down to wonder at the strange scene around me. People were crying or looking at the ground, all speaking in hushed voices.

I pulled open the front doors and headed towards my locker, looking around and puzzled by the similar scene inside.

My heart leapt when Sheila walked up beside me. She smiled.

"Hey, goofus." She put a hand on my arm. "We truly are dorks, aren't we?" She looked at the floor, then looked up at me, her eyes swimming in tears. "But I guess in the whole scheme of things, it doesn't really matter. Does it?" Her voice wavered, she sounded shaky.

I wanted her to go away. I didn't want to think about her, or Jane, or me. I didn't want to deal with her tears about what we'd done. And I didn't want any of my own slipping out.

"Are we okay?" she asked. "I mean, I know it was stupid and all, but in light of what's happened. . . well," she just trailed off.

Maybe, maybe not. I needed to figure things out. "We're fine," I said, glancing around me. "What the hell is going on around here, anyway?" I asked as I dialed my locker combination, glad to concentrate on something else.

Sheila stared at me in silence until I finally looked up. She bit her bottom lip. "You didn't hear, did you?"

"Hear what?" I popped my locker open.

"About Mona."

My heart dropped a little, and queasiness made me gulp. "Hear what about Mona?"

"She killed herself," Sheila said in a quiet voice. "Saturday night. At home. I heard she took a whole bottle of her mom's sleeping pills. They found her yesterday morning in her room. She was already dead."

An image of Mona laughing flitted through my head. Then I saw her at the musical tryouts, her sad eyes looking into mine for some sort of reassurance. I pictured Mona drunk, telling me she gave the best BJs in school. And I saw myself making out with her, followed by her blank look when I teased her later about the Halloween party. I envisioned her in Candy's bed, passed out. Then under Mac as he had sex with her.

"He always has sex with me when I'm drunk, Zack," I could hear her say.

"That son of a bitch." I slammed my fist against my locker.

Sheila turned her head.

"Do you think she found out about what I said to Mac outside, in front of everyone?" I asked, hoarsely.

Sheila lifted her shoulder and spoke softly. "I doubt it, Zack. She was obviously pretty messed up that night, and I don't know who would have told her."

"I feel like killing him."

Sheila frowned, looking at me as if I'd gone crazy.

I cringed at my choice of words. God! Mona was dead?

I thought about Friday night. It was the last time I saw her. I shook my head. I should have kept my mouth shut. Had I in some way contributed to this?

I inhaled deeply, not believing she was really gone. Mac would have to live with what he'd done. I hoped it would torture him for the rest of his life.

"Shit," I said.

"I know. It's horrible."

I glanced around. The scene made sense now. The kids hugging. All the crying.

"Have you seen Jane around?" For some crazy reason I needed to see if she was okay.

Sheila shook her head, her cheeks reddening a little. She looked away. "Not this morning."

"I have to find her." I looked Sheila in the eye. We could be embarrassed about our hormones later. Right now, we were dealing with a different reality.

Then a voice blared over the P.A. speakers. It was Mr.

Wright in his role as Vice Principal. He said something about Mr. Kirby being out for the day, and then asked everyone to report to the gymnasium immediately.

"I'll come with you to the gym. We'll look for her there." She waited while I closed my locker, and then she pulled me along to the gym. "Don't feel bad, okay, Zack? I don't want to lose you right now. You're still my best friend."

I patted her arm, and then we maneuvered through the halls. It was chaotic. Kids were either crying or talking to each other in hushed voices as they headed for the gym. We raced past everyone, still searching for Jane.

When we walked in the gym, I spotted her right away, despite all the kids who were gathering in clusters. Jane sat alone in the bleachers. Her head was down.

"Jane?" I said when I reached her.

She looked up. Her eyes were dry, but red. She stood and I went towards her.

"She's dead, Zack! Dead."

For the first time she made a move. She opened her arms and I stepped inside, feeling awkward with Sheila watching us.

"I know," I said into her hair. The scent of it filled my brain. It brushed softly against my cheek.

I held her for a moment and she didn't say a thing. Then she pulled away. She lifted her hand to greet Sheila, who sat down in the bleachers beside us, watching our awkward dance.

"Hi," Jane said, attempting a smile.

Sheila smiled back.

"David wants to talk to you," Jane told her. "He's really grateful, you know, for looking out for him."

Sheila looked around the gym. I felt a twinge in my belly and pretended it wasn't jealousy.

"He's not here," Jane said. "He's gone to—" She stopped. "I can trust you, right?"

Sheila rolled her eyes and nodded.

"Right! Well. He's gone to rehab for a couple of weeks. Somewhere out of town. My parents finally realized he's not going to get his drinking under control on his own, or with me chaperoning him. He needs a lot more than that."

Sheila nodded.

Jane continued, "He's going to be okay. I think he was sort of relieved to have it all explode the way it did. It forced something to happen, for them to finally do something. I think he was really ready." She took a deep breath. "Anyhow, he feels bad that he got you involved. He told me to say thanks, and that he'll tell you himself when he gets back. You guys were the best that night. You both were totally awesome."

Sheila turned bright red. I thought of her crushing on David and my insides stirred a little. Jane and I exchanged a look, and her face crumpled with sadness.

"God! I can't believe Mona. I mean, the last time we saw her. . . was at the party."

"I know." I'd have to tell Jane about what happened with Mac later. She'd hear about it anyway, since I'd pretty much announced it to the whole town. But not now—this wasn't the right time.

Jane sat down again, and I sat beside her. "We were best friends, you know. Up until eighth grade." Jane seemed almost to be talking to herself. Her eyes glazed over and she stared into space, remembering.

"She changed. So did you. It happens," I said, wanting to run out of the gym, far away from myself, and especially from Jane and Sheila.

Jane shook her head. "I know we did. But I just wish. . . well, we both handled things so differently. . . ."

"What do you mean, what things?" I asked.

She shook her head again. "Nothing." Her lips pressed into a thin line. I knew I wasn't going to get it out of her right now.

There was a crackling sound, and some static. Then we all looked towards the front of the gym at the stage where Mr. Wright stood with a microphone.

"Um, people. Quiet please. Everybody?"

The gym went quiet faster than I'd ever seen before.

"We've all heard the sad news about Mona Ryder. It's a shock. . . A real tragedy." A guidance counselor had been rounded up already, a thin man with a trimmed beard who looked like he spent all his free time running. He stood beside Mr. Wright.

"Well, I'll let Mr. Nelson take over from here. Mr. Nelson is a professional counselor. He will be joined by some of his colleagues soon and we'll break off into groups to give all of you a chance to talk about this." Even from the distance, I saw the relief on Mr. Wright's face. He looked too upset to even know what to say. Then he stepped back. The place was getting more crowded by the minute. Word had spread and kids were pouring in. I looked at Jane's sad face and put my arm around her shoulder. Sheila glanced up and smiled, nodding okay to me.

Mr. Nelson was doing a good job of offering comfort to the kids, but for some reason my eyes wandered to the doors of the gym. Mac walked in, accompanied as usual by his two shadows, Cole and Eddie. He stared directly at me. Across the gym, our eyes met and we held the gaze.

His eyes were dark and challenging, and he was staring me down. He seemed to have no shame. Not a twinge of guilt about what had happened to Mona. I glared back at him, repulsed by his lack of remorse. He must have seen something in my expression. He leaned over and whispered to Cole, still not taking his eyes off me.

I shook my head, turned from him and pulled Jane closer.

"You two stay as far away from Trevor MacDonald as is humanly possible," I warned.

Sheila and Jane turned to look at me, then followed my gaze to Mac.

"Forget about him!" Sheila said. "He's not worth your energy. I heard he's going to get questioned—"

"About what?" Jane asked.

Sheila and I exchanged a glance. There were a few things Jane didn't yet know. And a few she probably never would.

"Never mind. I want you to kick his hairy little ass," Jane spit out.

Sheila and I looked at her, and for a moment we were the same old friends we'd always been. We both started to laugh.

We stopped just as quickly, remembering where we were and why. A friend of Sheila's, another extra from the play, spotted us and came to sit beside her.

"You were at Candy's party?" she asked, looking at Sheila with a bit of reverence. "The last party Mona ever went to? I heard that Mac was having a threesome with her and another girl."

"That's totally not true. Don't be an idiot," Sheila snapped.

"Oh. Uh, I didn't think so. I mean, somebody else said it. I didn't really think it was true. Mona was always really nice to me." The girl's head hung a bit.

"Yeah, me, too." Sheila leaned over and whispered something to her friend.

Jane took the opportunity to bend forward to whisper to me. "Do you want to sneak out of here? Go somewhere we can talk?" she asked, quietly.

I nodded, feeling torn about which of them I owed my allegiance. I leaned the other way. "Sheila, we're going to take off and walk around outside."

Sheila nodded. She reached out and patted my arm, smiling at me. "It's okay, Zack." Then she turned back to her friend, filling her in on the details of Mona Ryder's last party.

Jane and I got up. She followed behind me as we slipped out of the bleachers. We kept close to the wall, squeezing around the other kids until we were out of the front door.

Kids were still flocking towards the gym. We navigated the hallways until we reached the doors leading outside.

Cars were pulling up to the front of the school, driven by concerned-looking parents who'd heard the news. A police car arrived next and I glanced back towards the gym.

"You want to wait and see if your parents are coming?" I asked, even though I wanted to get far away from the cops and from any questions they might have about Mac.

"No. They're at the rehab place with David."

I nodded, remembering David's predicament.

"Sheila has a crush on him," I said, feeling like a traitor.

"Yeah, I thought so. Well, he's going to need some good friends when he gets back."

I nodded again, wondering if Sheila still had a thing for him after what had happened between us.

"I can't believe Mona killed herself," I said.

A tear fell and slowly rolled down Jane's cheek. I glanced up and saw Mac's father rushing across the front lawn of the school, not even bothering to use the sidewalk.

"Let's walk," I said to Jane, nudging her along and away from the chaos of the school.

She nodded and we began to move. "She was my best friend, Zack."

"She was? What happened?"

Jane didn't say anything for a while. She looked around the parking lot as we crossed it.

"We never said a word about it. Not to anyone."

"About what?" I frowned, not sure what she was saying.

"We were in the eighth grade. I was babysitting for a kid who lived a couple blocks away. Mona came with me—we were inseparable then; and the family didn't mind it was both of us. The kids were little and they were sleeping when we got there." She stopped and took a deep breath.

"After the parents left, Mona got on the phone. She sort of idealized Candy then, since Candy was new at school that year. I didn't like her much, and we didn't really discuss it. Anyway, Mona and Candy had a bit of a thing for Trevor—Mac, I mean. Honestly, even I didn't think he was that bad back then. At least not until, well, later." She sighed, but I didn't speak. I waited for her to continue.

"About an hour or so later, the doorbell rang. I went to the door and cracked it open a bit. Mac pushed hard against it, knocking me against the wall. There were a couple of older guys with him. They pushed right past me and went down the hallway, past the family room and into the kitchen. They opened the fridge and cupboards, helping themselves to food and drinks. Then the three of them shared a beer."

I sucked in my breath as I waited for her to continue.

"They were whooping and hollering. When I think about it now, they were probably drunk. But I had no idea at the time. I mean, we were thirteen.

"I kept telling them to be quiet, to leave. I was so afraid they'd wake up the kids. They lit up a cigarette in the house, and I started freaking out. I told them to get out. They were being so loud and obnoxious. I was standing in the kitchen, yelling at them and almost crying. Mona was in the living room, trying to stop one of the guys from turning on the stereo.

"I heard Mona laugh a little, but she sounded kind of nervous. The guy, Richie, had stopped fooling with the stereo buttons and was playing with hers. Our eyes met for a moment, and I saw the fear in Mona's. But there was something else, too. Then I started crying.

"I didn't know what to do with these three crazy guys who were bigger than we were, and who just wouldn't leave. All I could think about was how much trouble I was going to get into." She stopped and gnawed on a fingernail before she spoke again.

"Mona started sounding more nervous, telling the guy to leave her alone. He had his hand up her shirt and his mouth buried in her neck. She was leaning back, trying to get away. I yelled at him, then started down the steps to the living room. But that's when the other guy grabbed me. His name was Terry. He held my arms behind my back."

She made a face and shook her head. "At first, Mac seemed almost confused. I was asking him to help us, but the guy holding Mona was egging him on. He grabbed Mona and ripped open the zipper on her jeans, then stuck his hand down her pants. Then he told Mac to have a feel."

I swallowed, my anger building.

"She tried to get away but she couldn't. She was always tiny and they outweighed her by at least forty or fifty pounds."

My hands clenched into a fist.

"Then the guy holding me called Mac, and told him to do it to me, too, to compare. And he did. He stuck his hands down my pants. And then the guy holding Mona yelled. She'd bitten him or something. Mac went back to Mona while the other guy held me. Mona, well, she was a lot more developed than I was. So Mac took her shirt off. And then he started doing other really rude things to her. I was crying and wanted to close my eyes, but I couldn't let Mona be all alone. Mona was crying, too, and finally I just lost it. I started screaming, loud. To hell with waking the kids.

"Mac freaked! He looked me in the eye, and then he kind of jumped off Mona. He told the other guys they'd better go, before someone heard me screaming. He looked right at me and he said, 'You totally deserve this, you little cock tease.' And then they finally were gone. They just pushed both of us onto the floor, and then they took off."

Jane stopped talking for a second, a little out of breath. "Mona put on her clothes and went home. I had to stay, of course. I couldn't leave the kids by themselves. I cleaned up the mess and opened up all the windows, trying to clear out the cigarette smell. And when the couple got back, I went home without telling anyone what had happened. I thought it was all my fault. And Mona probably thought it was hers. We never talked about what happened that night. Not ever.

"After that, she started hanging out with Candy and the wilder crowd. She started drinking, and eventually she and I just stopped talking to each other."

I reached for her and pulled her close. She let me hold her for a while. She kept talking into my chest. "That's when I dyed my hair black. My parents hated it, but since I'd never done anything bad before, they couldn't do much about it. They were too busy worrying about David to really worry too much about me. But I knew I didn't want blonde hair anymore. I didn't want boys looking at me like that ever again."

I held her tighter for a moment, and then I stepped back. I took a breath and told her about the scene I'd found when I went back to check on Mona. I wanted to tell her the truth, and I told her about the fight with Mac. But I didn't mention the part with Sheila on the ride home.

Jane's eyes filled with tears when she heard what Mac had done to Mona.

"I'd like to kill him myself," she said.

"You wouldn't look good in stripes," I joked.

I pulled her close and breathed in the fresh scent of her hair. God! I liked this girl. I really did.

"You should tell the police. About what happened."

She shook her head and pushed me away. "No. I mean, it wouldn't really change anything. And I don't need everyone to know. I mean it, no."

"Okay." I understood. I reached for her and we were still hugging when I heard my name being called.

"Zachary? Zachary!"

It was my mom. She came running and then slowed down as she got closer.

"I heard about that girl. Are you okay?"

I nodded.

"You?" she asked Jane. I was glad she included Jane.

"Jane and Mona were friends," I told her.

She nodded. "Your parents coming to get you?"

Jane shook her head. "They're busy with my brother."

"Do you want to come with Zachary and me? We could all go somewhere to talk. I'll take you kids to the store. You can chat with Aunt Diane and me about it. Would that help?" She wrung her hands, not really sure what to do.

"Thanks, Mom. But I don't know. I think we'll stay here for now. They're kind of having us gather in the gym for counseling. I'd kind of like to go back there and listen."

Mom nodded and wrung her hands some more. For the first time she was out of her element. Claire would have left me and run to my mom for a hug of reassurance. Jane would never think of doing something like that.

"Okay. Well, can I get you kids anything?"

"Mom, it's okay. Go to work. I'm fine. We're fine."

"I'll pick you up after school. If you need me, you call, okay?"

"Uh, yeah. Actually, I think I'm going to go to the rink, Mom. There's a practice at 4:30. Jane can probably drive me."

I glanced at Jane. She nodded. When I turned back to Mom, a look of joy washed across her face, and then she looked a little guilty.

"Oh?" she said in a calm voice that didn't fool me at all.

"Yeah. I'm going to lace up. My equipment is at the rink. I'll do a little skating. Might as well get ready to get back in the game."

She nodded her head, her eyes shining with emotion.

She smiled at Jane, in case she was the reason for the sudden change in my attitude.

She rocked on her heels and then smiled, and finally said goodbye.

When she was gone, Jane turned to me. "You're going back to the team?"

"I am going to kill him in a completely legal way."

Jane nodded, her eyes wide. "Yes. Hurt him!"

"I think I might have a little already. His reputation, anyhow. Besides, this is only hockey, but I'll do what I can on the ice, where it matters to Mac. We'll see what I can do off the ice, too."

A few days later, Mr. Wright smiled at me as I walked backstage during the *Grease* rehearsal.

"You're sure you want to go through with this, Zack?" he said, grinning at me. "There's still time to bail. This is only the dress rehearsal, and if I had to, I could find someone else to dance with the T-Birds and do the guitar solo."

He glanced down at the clipboard in his hand, frowning as he studied his notes. He'd gathered everyone from the play together before rehearsal, and we decided to dedicate the play as a tribute to Mona's memory.

"You know, for a teacher, you like to taunt me a lot. Maybe I'm a little nervous."

He glanced up from the clipboard and winked. "You'll be great, Zack. I'm not worried about you."

I hesitated before I spoke again. "I have a hockey game, you know, on opening night."

He nodded. "Big game for your team, win or lose."

I shrugged. "It's okay. I'm used to pressure."

Mr. Wright studied me and then spoke again, his teasing tone gone, his voice more serious. "You know, I really can get someone else if you have stuff to do after the game. You know, if it's too much. I know you're under a lot of pressure."

"No—I'll be here. There's enough time for me to make it back after the game."

Backstage, kids were scrambling. Everyone was in costume. Cassandra hurried by, waving at me. She was playing one of the Pink Ladies. She was clearly the best singer, but someone thinner got the part of Sandy. Cassandra hadn't been too upset about it, but Jane was hopping mad.

Mr. Wright nodded and waved at Cassandra, assuming her greeting had been for him. "Okay, it's your call. Don't let us down, Zachary. If you commit to it, you've got to get back here for the play. This is as important to the cast and me as your hockey game is to you."

I grinned at him. "Maybe this is more important: my new career. Zack Chase, actor. Maybe next year, I'll be the star of the show."

"You could do it if you wanted. Your voice is good enough for a lead." He started towards the entrance of the stage.

He waved his hand and called over his shoulder. "You'll figure it all out. You have to decide what you want to do, Zachary, *you*. It's up to you and nobody else."

He disappeared into a circle of teenagers who were fretting and jumpy from stage fright.

Decisions. That's what it always boiled down to. I needed to figure out what I wanted. Myself. I smiled.

Before any of that, I knew I had a few things to do first.

I decided I would walk. The police station wasn't too far from the school. And I had something important to talk to the police about.

CHAPTER 12

Whack.

I was back.

A kid had checked me and it hurt like hell, but I just kept skating, ignoring the pain. I expected the other team to exploit my weakness. We were in the playoffs now and it was all about winning. And winning was what Zachary Chase had been born to do.

I skated after the puck, my eyes focused on the little black object I lusted after. Once I felt it on my stick, I knew no one could stop me. I would barrel over anything in my way. Without even realizing it, while I'd been off the ice, the whole time I'd been waiting to score.

The guys on the team still seemed kind of shocked at my resurrection. They'd seen me play before, but never like this. After Mona's death I woke up. I creamed Mac once for her, another time for Jane, and gave him a bonus creaming for me, and then I played hard. I had points to make; I wasn't kidding around anymore.

Now, weeks later, the Huskies were in the playoffs.

I'd helped to make it happen. Not single-handedly, but I was a force to be reckoned with.

This was it. The playoffs. There were two minutes left in the second period, and we were behind 2-1. If we lost this game, that was it, we'd be eliminated. There was only one little problem with that. I wasn't finished playing hockey! This time I had to be the victor.

My skates dug into the ice, spraying slush as I flew across the surface, my breathing fast and urgent. Focusing on the puck, I ignored the opponent racing me. I hustled and saw David skate up from the right, beating me to the puck. He glanced over, and I imagined his goofy trademark smile. Then, like there was a magnetic force between our sticks, he passed the puck in a beautiful straight-on delivery. And it was right where it belonged, on the end of my stick. It was my puck now. I focused on the net, eyeing the goalie, and gauging in nanoseconds where to slap my little captive.

Then suddenly, out of nowhere, another player skated at me, threatening my on-target shot. I heard my name being called, just as Mac skated in. Now, *he* was the one in the position to score. I took a quick glance at the goalie, then made my split-second decision. I chose to take a risk.

Screw you, Mac, I thought.

I fixed my eye on the speck between the goalie's glove and the net, then slapped at the puck with all my might. I watched in slow-mo as it ripped apart molecules on its way. The goalie's glove reached up, while his black Cooper skates rose off the ice. He lunged his bulky, padded body to try and block the puck's trip towards the white threads of his net. For what seemed like forever I held my breath.

Then the green light went off and the buzzer sounded. I lifted my stick in the air, hollering at the top of my lungs.

In the background I heard the crowd going crazy, cheering, stomping their feet on the metal bleachers. The noise sounded like gunshots, and filled my ears like a beautiful song.

"Yes!" I shouted, pumping my stick in the air with both hands. Score!

I lowered my stick and took a quick look at the bleachers. Sheila jumped up and down in the front row, whacking on the glass with both hands. She'd taken the day off from the canteen, just so she could watch the action close up. Her face glowed, she looked beautiful. I searched the stands for Jane, who I spotted a few rows up. She was laughing, clapping, and there was no book in sight.

My mom and aunt were in the front with Sheila, jumping up and down, hugging each other and waving to me on the ice. I smiled as I skated towards the bench, getting slaps on the back from my line-up and the guys coming to replace us. But the game wasn't over—not yet.

Before I reached the bench, Mac's blades tore up behind me, spraying me with ice.

"Hey. Chase. We're a team, remember, asshole? I could have had that goal. I was clear."

I turned. "I don't know, Mac. Your shots on goal average is pretty grim. Not such a problem with mine." I said it low, so only he could hear me. Then I opened the door and hopped inside our team's box.

Coach Cal slapped the back of my helmet. "Good goal, Zack. We need a couple more like that."

I didn't answer, but I couldn't sit down yet. I leaned forward watching the play. The water boy, the coach's son, handed me a water bottle.

"Good play, Zack Attack," he said, a little bit of hero worship in his voice.

"Thanks, Blair," I grinned at him, taking the water.

"You've been on fire since you got back," he added, eyes wide.

A few players down, Mac cursed from his seat on the bench. He had a right to be bitter. While he'd been dealing with the police and accusations about what he'd done to the girls in town, especially the one who killed herself, I'd rallied the team and done everything a good captain should do. Except I wasn't captain; Mac was. And he was a captain with problems.

Fortunately for him, the police questioning led to nothing. Even with what I'd witnessed they couldn't do much. It was my word against his. Mona wasn't around to press charges, and nothing could be proved.

I didn't know if he ever found out I'd told the police what I'd witnessed. And I didn't care if he found out. As it stood, I hadn't heard anything from him or his dad. But I was sure there had to be a reason. There were rumors floating around the school about other girls he'd molested, and Mac was lying pretty low and keeping quiet. Still, he was a free man. I imagined that before long, he'd be back to his usual cocky, obnoxious attitude. I hoped he'd actually learned something, but somehow I doubted it. Not everyone learns from their mistakes.

Blair waited reverently for me to finish my water, and then handed me a clean towel. The horn blew, signaling the end of the second period. As the team retired to the locker room, I hung back on the bench, waiting for everyone to leave. Mac was pacing the locker room by the time I got there.

"We're a team, loser. Try passing the puck once in a while," he snapped at me, as soon as I walked in.

"He's doing a pretty good job of scoring goals, Mac. Which is more than anyone can say for you," David yelled from the bench where he was slumped, trying to catch his breath.

"Screw off, Parker, you alky," Mac shouted back.

"Cut it out," Coach Cal jumped in. "Mac, go sit down and cool off. The reason we're even still in this game is because of Chase, so keep it quiet."

"No way. Parker is smoking on the wing," I piped up, before Mac could say anything else. I sat beside David and punched his shoulder. "Being sober agrees with your game, bro." I smiled to show I was kidding around.

"Screw that," he said. "I'm so bored, I could spit."

Candy had officially dumped him, right before Mona's funeral. David sat with Cassandra, Sheila, Jane, and me at the service, much too involved in his own drama to notice Sheila smiling at him. They let him out of rehab for a couple of days to attend the funeral, and he seemed surprisingly committed to not drinking.

The turnout at the funeral was huge, with standing room only at the church. I think Mona would have been surprised to see how many kids cared. Who knows, maybe they were just curious. I guess when someone so young dies, it makes people reach out to each other, probably for comfort.

There in the locker room, I continued teasing David.

"Yeah, but you play hockey. You don't need a life!" I needled him again.

"Quiet, you two," Coach Cal broke into our conversation to give us a heartfelt pep talk. I glanced over at Mac, then, grinning dramatically, I stood up and led the team in a cheer. Mac flipped me the bird as I yelled. I winked at him as the team roared in response and we all raced back to the ice.

The period got under way fast. With the game tied 2-2, both teams hustled to get the puck in the net. We swore at each other, and dug our sticks into vulnerable body parts when the refs weren't looking. We sweated, working it, but no one could score a goal in a clear net.

Before I knew it, there was less than two minutes left. It was still a tie game. My line poured out on the ice: David, Mac, the defensemen, and me.

"Zack Attack! Zack Attack! Zack Attack!"

I heard the chanting from the crowd. I glanced over as I skated to the blue line for the puck drop. Sheila jumped up and down on the bench, leading the crowd in the cheer. I stopped skating for a moment, just watching. Jane sat quietly in the crowd behind her, almost as if she were holding her breath. I laughed to myself, watching their different reactions for a moment, until I heard the ref blowing his whistle.

"Get over here, kid, or I'll give you a penalty for holding up the game," he yelled at me.

I smiled and skated over, sliding past Mac. "Pass the puck," he hissed.

"Bite me," I said, and moved on.

The ref lifted his hand and dropped the puck. I jabbed in and stole it. With the puck on my stick, I skated away from the others, over the blue line. In the clear, I took a shot.

The goalie leapt across the net like a spider, trapping the puck in his glove. Then he threw it back on the ice, putting it back into play, just as an opposing player zoomed past and scooped it up. I took off after him and dug my stick in, managing to steal the puck and head back to my target. I looked up. The goalie had his net covered, while a defenseman blocked my shot. From my spot, I couldn't get a clear shot. I glanced over my shoulder. Mac hovered to my right, out in the open. From his better position, he had a decent shot.

I made a split-second decision. Taking a deep breath and saying a mini-prayer, I shot the puck his way.

Mac landed the pass and brought his stick back. He fired it, making the goal. The horn went off and the game was over!

Our teammates poured out off the bench and onto the ice, jumping on top of Mac. I skated slowly towards the pile of players.

David spotted me. "Zack Attack!" He shouted in his big baritone voice.

Someone else joined in. "Zack Attack!"

The crowd joined the chant: "Zack Attack! Zack Attack!"

David leapt in front of me and held out his arms to keep the guys from jumping on me. "Don't forget his ribs! Don't jump on him!" he shouted.

Mac got off the ice and skated over. He stuck out his hand. "Good pass."

I looked down at his palm. "It was for the team, Mac. Not you. You're still a giant asshole."

I didn't shake his hand, but skated away towards the bench to get a drink of water.

I watched from the boards as Mac accepted the league trophy, for a big beautiful hunk of victory. He hoisted it in the air, then did a triumphant lap around the rink. I viewed it from the side, smiling to myself.

The game was over. We'd won. I just wanted to finish shaking hands with the other team so I could leave, get changed, and get to my play on time.

In the locker room the guys hooted and hollered. I got into my clothes in record time, not talking to anyone. I threw my hockey bag over my shoulder, then headed for the door.

"Great game! Good job!" Guys called out.

I nodded as I hurried out of the locker room.

In the hallway, my mom and aunt started squealing and jumping up and down when they saw me. I let them act silly without saying a word. My mom loved her hockey. I didn't understand everything about her, but she deserved the win, too.

I bent down and hugged her when she ran at me.

She spoke right in my ear. "I'm so proud of you, Zachary. Your dad would be so proud of you, too."

I smiled and straightened. Yeah. Well, maybe he would have. Maybe.

Behind my mom, a man stared at the two of us. I didn't recognize him, but he walked forward when he saw that I'd noticed him.

"Zachary Chase?" he said as he approached. "Mrs. Chase?"

I nodded. He stuck out his hand. "I'm Dean Johnson, a recruiter for Boston College Eagles. I'd love to talk to you about your plans for the next couple years if you've got a minute."

My mom let out a little yelp of pleasure.

He pulled out a card and handed it to me. I looked over his shoulder. His mouth moved but I didn't hear the words. Jane approached slowly. With her crazy dyed hair and her dark outlined eyes, she looked like the anti-Puck. I looked down to read the words on her shirt. In tiny black letters it read, "My IQ is bigger."

I laughed.

David came up behind her, grinning. I glanced over and saw Sheila walking beside him, laughing. She caught my eye and we grinned at each other. I nodded my head towards David slightly and raised my eyebrows suggestively. She stuck out her tongue and I smiled again.

Maybe it'd been a mistake, Sheila and me. I watched as she and David veered off towards the exit, wondering if they would become a couple. I couldn't imagine it, but who was I to say?

In the background, Dean talked on about scholarships and prospects, and where I wanted to go in the future. On one level my brain buzzed with excitement. Because for the first time in my life, I knew without question that I needed to play hockey. And I was completely okay with it. I'd already dealt with everything a professional hockey career meant, and would deal with it in my own way if that's where hockey led me. But I'd deal with it my way. Not my dad's.

Dean noticed me staring at Jane and stopped talking as she approached.

I glanced at him. "Excuse me, Mr. Johnson. I don't want to be rude, but I have an obligation to be somewhere else right now." I turned to my mom. She took a quick look at Jane, then back at Dean and me. Her face was hard to read, but the corner of her mouth turned up slightly.

"Mom, I gotta go. I want to talk—I do, but I really have to go." I glanced at Dean. "Can you discuss this with my mom? Maybe we can all have lunch or something tomorrow?"

Dean's face looked puzzled but he nodded.

"I have to go now."

Neither of them answered, but I didn't wait. I squeezed past them to reach for Jane. She'd been watching me, her eyes uncertain. Then I heard Mac's dad behind us, trying to interrupt my mom and Dean.

"No thanks, sir. I'm only here to talk to Zachary Chase," Dean said firmly, while Mac's dad spouted off.

"You hear that?" Jane asked me.

Mr. MacDonald's face turned red. It didn't seem

healthy for a man his age. Mac stood beside him, just as tall, but slouched as if he'd just lost his dog.

"He scored the winning goal," Mr. MacDonald said, loud enough for everyone in the arena to hear.

"Off an awesome pass by Zachary." Dean spoke in a powerful voice that carried through the place. "Besides, we don't even look at kids with bad reputations like his. Word gets around, Mr. MacDonald. He's not the kind of kid we want." He turned his back to Mac's dad, and continued talking with my mom.

I watched as Mr. MacDonald dragged Mac out of the arena.

For a moment Mac turned. We exchanged a brief look. He turned away quickly, but for a second I thought I saw relief. It had to be tough, always having his dad harp on him like that.

I wondered if there was something else Mac wanted to do with his life. Besides hockey and abusing women.

I watched him leave, wondering what my dad would have done if he'd been here tonight. I wondered if he'd like Jane, or if I'd tell him about my mixed-up feelings about Jane, Sheila, and hockey. Nah. Probably not.

"I almost feel sorry for him," I said, as Mac left the arena with his head down. And then I thought of what he'd done to Jane and Mona. I turned to Jane. "I'm sorry. That sounded terrible. He doesn't deserve pity after what he's done."

In my book that kind of behavior had no excuse. Everyone has choices. I thought of Mona, and the play she wouldn't be in. I tried to imagine the person she might have become, if only she'd stuck it out. She'd been messed with and was seriously messed up, but she'd had a lot of potential.

I truly wished I hadn't trashed her dignity by telling people what I'd seen. If I could only take things back, I would. I guess that's true of mostly everybody. Probably even Mac.

"I went to the police, you know," Jane said softly, breaking into my thoughts. "I went before the game. I told them about what Mac did to Mona and me that time in eighth grade."

I grabbed her hand, searching her eyes. "You did?"

She nodded. "I don't know if it'll make any difference. It happened a long time ago. But I still wanted to tell them. You know, for Mona. And I did it for me. I'm sick of feeling guilty about it. If we'd said something sooner, things could have turned out different. Maybe Mona would still be in the play."

"Let's get out of here," I whispered in Jane's ear. "If we don't go now, we'll never make it in time."

Jane glanced at me, and then over at my mom and Dean. I followed her gaze. Their body language looked interesting; it looked as if they were flirting. Sparks were flying between them that didn't seem to have anything to do with my future career in hockey.

"She'll kill you for taking off."

"Nah, she'll forgive me." I automatically glanced around looking for Sheila, forgetting for a second she'd left with David. She'd be at the play. We'd talk about it sometime, Sheila and me. About what happened between us that night. Or maybe not.

Jane punched me on the arm. "Let's go."

"Zachary?"

I turned around. My aunt studied Jane and me.

"We've got to go now," I told her. "I've got to be at school for the curtain in an hour. I have a part in *Grease*."

Aunt Diane nodded. She smiled a conspiring smile. "Leave your equipment bag here. I'll bring it to your mom when she's done flirting with that scout."

I shot a look at my mom. She twirled a piece of hair around her finger, smiling at Dean with a smile I'd never seen before.

"Hurry! Go! I'll remind her about your show once she's done mesmerizing the scout." Aunt Diane grinned. "She'll have you signed with the biggest team in the world by the end of your performance."

"You know, she always did steal the cute ones," she said in mock anger. "First good-looking man to show up in Haletown in two solid years, and your mother already has him in her clutches."

We glanced over at mom, then back at each other. Aunt Diane giggled like a schoolgirl.

"Go on, Zachary. This is good for her. It's about time you both start living your lives."

I gave my aunt a quick hug.

"We're both so proud of you," Aunt Diane beamed.

"I guess hockey really is in my blood."

"It's *your* blood, Zachary," Aunt Diane said. "And your father would have wanted you to do what makes you happy, you know. You. It's not about him. It's not even about your mother. He was a good man, no matter what."

I nodded. "I hope so. You know, I tried denying how much I love hockey. Because I'm afraid of turning out like him. But I guess I already am." I spoke to Aunt Diane, but kept my eyes on Jane.

"You're only fifteen. I still don't know what I want all the time, and I'm pushing thirty, or so." My aunt laughed.

I smiled. I had choices to make. That much was true. I studied Aunt Diane for a minute. She was the spitting image of my mom.

"I'm nothing like him."

"Of course you are. But you're not him. You're Zachary," Aunt Diane said proudly.

"Yeah, I guess." I turned to Jane. "We have to go or we'll be late."

Aunt Diane nodded. "We'll be there. Ten bucks says Mr. Scout Man will be there, too." She smiled. "Knock 'em dead, kids."

Jane and I hurried out of the arena.

"I'm nervous," I said to Jane.

Jane squeezed my fingers. "You'll be fine."

"I know."

After the play, I'd think more about what I wanted in life. What I'd tell Jane. And what I wouldn't.

But for right now, I had a part to play. I took her hand and we left.

Acknowledgments

To Mom and Dad for making me grow up in a hockey rink. Thanks, sort of.
To Evelyn Fazio, editor extraordinaire, who believed in Zack's story.
Kathryn Green, the agent who made the match,
and
To Kyle MacLeod for his eyes and his advice.
And to the many writers at Verla Kay's Blueboard and my lovely LJ community. You know who you are and you totally rock.
Thanks.